WILD
TIMOTHY

WILD
TIMOTHY

Gary L. Blackwood

ATHENEUM   1987   NEW YORK

Atheneum
Macmillan Publishing Company
866 Third Avenue, New York, NY 10022
Collier Macmillan Canada, Inc.

Type set by Haddon Craftsmen, Allentown, Pennsylvania
Printed and bound by Fairfield Graphics, Fairfield, Pennsylvania
Designed by Jean Krulis
First Edition

10 9 8 7 6 5 4 3 2 1

Library of Congress Cataloging-in-Publication Data

Blackwood, Gary L.
Wild Timothy.

SUMMARY: Thirteen-year-old Timothy, more interested in reading than in physical activity, reluctantly accompanies his enthusiastic father on a camping trip and, when he accidently becomes lost in the woods, discovers that he is capable of surviving on his own.
[1. Survival—Fiction. 2. Fathers and sons—Fiction.
3. Self-reliance—Fiction. 4. Camping—Fiction]
I. Title.
PZ7.B5338Wi   1987   [Fic]   87-937
ISBN 0-689-31352-7

FOR GARETH,
WHO HAS ALWAYS FELT "COMFOR'BLE"
IN THE WOODS

WILD
TIMOTHY

ONE

THE RED NYLON of the tent was closing in on him, nearly black in the darkness. For the third or fourth time Timothy slipped his arm out of the sleeping bag and reached up to reassure himself that the tent was still where it should be, three feet or so above his head, and still stretched taut. The fabric felt damp, coated with his moist breath and his father's. Timothy felt suffocated, like he was breathing their old expended breath over and over again. Squirming half out of the sleeping bag, he lifted one corner of the tent flap and inhaled the cold air, which smelled of pine needles and moldy leaves. Then, chilled, he crawled back inside the mummy bag, wishing his father had let him bring his pajamas.

The tent fabric acted something like a greenhouse, closing them in with their stale breath, yet failing to keep out the presence of the forest. It effectively screened out all the fresh air, but somehow every slightest noise seemed magnified, as though the tent walls vibrated in time with each owl's hoot and bobcat's scream. Timothy reached up to touch the nylon roof once more, then turned over and closed his eyes, waiting for sleep.

Just when he had gotten more or less used to the various noises of the woods and had begun to drift off, he heard a new sound: a guttural, bearlike, whuffing sound. Timothy's eyelids opened abruptly, and he lay still as a corpse, his breath coming rapid and shallow, listening for the sound to be repeated, or maybe for the flimsy walls of the tent to collapse under the weight of a huge paw. Was this how it would end for him—thirteen years of life snuffed out by a bear?

The ranger they had talked to had said there were still bears in some areas, so they were to be sure and hang their food supply from a tree branch ten feet or more above the ground. How big did that make the bears then, if eight feet, or nine, was not beyond their reach?

A twig snapped somewhere nearby, and Timothy held his breath. After a long moment, he heard the whuffing sound again, almost in his ear. He let out his breath in an explosive sigh, realizing with a combination of relief and disgust that what he had heard was his father giving an abbreviated snore. Rolling over on his back, Timothy untangled the sleeping bag, which had insisted on rolling with him, and lay looking up at the roof of the tent, watching for it to grow red again in the first daylight, wishing he were staring up at the familiar cracks and stains on the ceiling of his bedroom.

That ceiling was a world of its own, nearly as real to him—and more friendly—than the usual one in which he slept and ate meals and read books and went to school. It was a map of a world, really, depicting an enormous and mysterious water-stain continent with cracked-plaster rivers running through it. In the border lands that extended down one wall lay a peeled-wallpaper lake, and dusky forests that, looked at in a certain way, were merely a pattern in the wallpaper.

The thing the map did not reveal was whether or not there were people on that island continent, dwelling in clearings in its forests, navigating its rivers. Timothy felt there must be, though they were of a different sort from those who populated his own world. Probably they were a simple, easygoing people, who picked their food from trees and sat around telling stories. But then, of course, you could never tell much from a map. The Adirondacks, too, were no more than a greenish pattern when looked at on the New York map in the road atlas, just as Elmira was nothing more than an orange blot.

When his father had first proposed the camping trip, neither Timothy nor his mom had liked the idea, but his mom said, pointing at the map, "Oh, well, look— there are towns and everything up there. It's not like you'd be in the middle of nowhere."

"Towns?" Timothy said sarcastically. "Oh, sure. I'll bet North Wilmurt is a biggie."

Unperturbed, his father ran a finger along the red

veins of road, tracing the best route. "We're not going there to window-shop. We're going to camp—to rough it, to commune with nature."

His mother sighed. "I don't know, Jerry. Isn't it cold at night in August up there? How are you going to stay warm? You know how easily Timmy gets sick. He always has."

"You stay warm by cutting wood and burning it. It'll be good for him, build him up a little." He punched Timothy's arm playfully.

"Ow," Timothy said.

Something was nudging his arm again, now, and he sat upright in the mummy bag, alarmed. It must be the bear. To his surprise, the interior of the tent was glowing red with daylight. The flap was lifted, and his father was grinning in at him. "Jumpy, aren't you?"

"What time is it?" Timothy mumbled.

"Time to get up. You want to catch fish, you've got to get an early start."

"What if I don't want to?"

His father shrugged. "Then I guess you don't eat."

"You mean we're gonna have *fish* for breakfast?"

"It'll sound good once you've been up for an hour or two." His father finished pulling on thigh-high waders and clomped off to see to his fishing tackle.

"Fish for breakfast," Timothy grumbled again, and, rooting his glasses out from among his clothes, slipped them on and checked his watch. "Six o'clock! Shoot!" How did his father expect him to get "built up" if he

6

didn't let him get any sleep? He considered flopping back into the sleeping bag, but he knew his father would just come back and rout him out again, and this time he'd be yelling. It probably wasn't worth it. Besides, he promised his mom to try and get along. "He's making an effort," she had said. "You've got to make an effort, too."

"Couldn't he find some other way?" Timothy had said. "Why couldn't he just be home once in a while?"

She hadn't answered. But he knew the answer anyway, because they'd had the same argument any number of times. It was the business. When you owned a construction company, you had to hustle, or somebody else got the job.

Hustle. Bustle. Muscle. Timothy kicked the sleeping bag off and climbed into his clothes, trying to hustle. It was hard to do within the confines of the tent, but if he stepped outside, he'd get covered with leaves and dirt. Finally, he crammed his feet into his new hiking boots and emerged from the tent like a fledgling butterfly from its cocoon, just as his father was heading for the tent again, prepared to yell.

His father should have looked ridiculous in the clumsy waders and worn vest and floppy hat with artificial flies stuck in the band, but he didn't—he looked like he'd just stepped off the cover of *Field and Stream*. Some people just looked that way all the time, like they were living in a commercial. His brother, Kevin, was the same way, except where his dad belonged in a Budweiser commercial, or maybe Wranglers, Kevin

7

was more the Mountain Dew type, or Pepsi: clean-cut, always grinning, always acting like he'd never even heard of dandruff or bad breath or acne. The only commercial that could conceivably have contained Timothy was maybe the one for that video game where the kids were all kind of fat, or nerdy-looking. Not that he was fat, exactly, just a little on the flabby side. He didn't get all that exercise that the guys in commercials got: Chasing after girls who stole their cowboy hats and jumping headlong into mountain pools and playing soccer.

Kevin played soccer; in fact, he was already a rising star at Syracuse in his freshman year. He would have been just as good, probably, at baseball or track, but they didn't seem as much like a commercial.

His father looked his disheveled, rumpled son over. "Where's your pole?"

"In the car, I guess."

"Well, don't just stand there—go get it. It's getting late in the day for good fishing."

Late? Timothy said to himself as he trotted to the Jeep. If it was any earlier, the fish couldn't see the bait. When he got to the vehicle, he realized he needed the keys to open the rear door, so he trotted back to where his father stood flicking his fly rod impatiently. "What now?"

"Keys," said Timothy. With them in hand, he returned and opened the back of the Jeep. As he lifted his pole out from behind the spare tire, he saw that a foot-long piece of it had been broken off, presumably by the closing door; it dangled on the end of the fishing line. "Oh, crap," he groaned, and stuck the broken piece back on the end of the rod. It promptly fell off again.

As he started away from the Jeep, he noticed his father gesturing, but he was almost halfway to him before he understood the message. "The door! Close the door! And bring the keys!" Timothy sighed and turned back. This was going to be some terrific day.

His father long-sufferingly whittled off the pole at the second eyelet, and they hiked through about a mile of dew-wet grass to the river. The original plan had been to camp at Moose Lake, where his father had gone on a fishing trip years before, with his own dad, Timothy's grandfather. But things had changed in the intervening years—Moose Lake and a lot of others were gradually losing their fish population, thanks to acid rain produced by pollutants borne on the wind from Midwestern factory smokestacks. So they settled for a spot on the Independence River.

Unfortunately, if there were still fish in the river, they chose not to reveal themselves today. After nearly two hours of wading around and flinging every sort of fly in his arsenal into every square inch of a hundred-yard stretch of river, while Timothy stood shivering in his wet hiking boots on the bank and plied the water with a single bedraggled spinner, his father gave up, growling, "I knew we should have got an earlier start." Back in camp, after trying for some time to start a fire with damp branches, they lit up the Coleman stove and fried slices of bread and canned lunch meat and discussed how early they should rise the following morning.

After that, there didn't seem to be much to talk about. But then that was the way it always was. Even in those few hours a day that his father spent with the family, he did most of his talking to Timothy's mom —about money—or to Kevin about ball—either foot- or base-, depending on the season. For a while Timothy had tried watching the pro games on TV, but the first time he spoke knowingly about the New York Mets' great defense, they laughed at him, and he gave up and went back to reading Robert Louis Stevenson, waiting fiercely for the moment when one of them would slip up and say, "Stevenson? Didn't he write *A Tale of Two Cities?*" He'd laugh so hard.

But of course they'd never said any such thing, and even if they had, they would not have been the least embarrassed. They would only have turned it around somehow so that Timothy would be the one to feel stupid for even caring who wrote what.

As he sat on a log, sweating and swatting at gnats, watching his father tie new and more irresistible flies, Timothy wished for a cold drink and a copy of *The Black Arrow,* but his father had flatly refused to bring along such decadent luxuries as ice and books. It would be interesting to see if the old man could really make it through an entire week without a cold beer. Well, anyway, that was one thing that could be said for roughing it—it made you really appreciate the small things you always took for granted.

Early in the afternoon, bored to exhaustion, Timothy dug up a few worms and went to dangle them in the river for want of anything better to do. After ten minutes, when nothing had taken his bait, he laid the pole in the grass and leaned up against a sapling to daydream. No sooner had he settled himself than the shortened end of the pole dipped toward the water. He lunged for it and, reeling furiously, pulled in a small but very feisty sunfish. Once he had it off the hook, he didn't quite know what to do with it, so he laid it carefully in the shade and baited the hook again. There was an instant replay, and he pulled in the fish's twin, then, within a half-hour, four of its brothers and sisters. Half proud and half plain surprised, he carried his catch back to camp gingerly in his arms, having neglected to bring along a creel or stringer. Grinning sheepishly, he called out as he entered the clearing, "Um . . . look at this, Dad. I caught our dinner!"

"You what?" His father turned irritably from a fly he was fooling with. "You caught something?" Timothy crouched down to show him the gaping, glassy-eyed fish. "Oh. Just sunfish." His father turned back to his fly. "They're not worth the trouble to clean."

"Well . . . I—I'll clean them, if you show me how."

"I said it wasn't worth the trouble. You should've just thrown them back."

"It's *something* anyhow. It's fish, isn't it?"

11

"Ahh, tomorrow we'll catch some bass. That's real fish."

Timothy looked down at the dead sunfish. "Well . . . what should I do with them, then?"

"I don't know. Just toss them off in the bushes someplace. Better take them way off, where they won't attract wild animals." He glanced up at Timothy. "And you better wash out that shirt, too, or it's going to smell."

When he had disposed of the fish and washed the shirt, Timothy wandered around aimlessly for a while. Finally, finding himself on the overgrown logging trail that answered for a road, he ambled down to the Jeep and slid into the passenger seat. Inside, it was like a small man-made oasis, clean and comfortable and sheltered. Sometimes at home he went out and sat in the Jeep or the station wagon and, leafing through the road atlas, pretended he was en route to some other place, somewhere more interesting—California, maybe, or Florida. Almost always it was someplace near the ocean. But not a remote place. A place with great stretches of yellow beach, and orange and banana trees you could pick the fruit from.

This time, though, he didn't bother to pull the atlas out of the glove compartment—he was pretending the Jeep sat in the driveway at home and that, anytime he wanted, he could go indoors and pour a Coke and pick up *The Man in the Iron Mask.* It was a difficult thing to imagine, even with his eyes closed, for instead of the reassuring sound of the neighbor's dog barking, he heard the wind in the grass and the occasional eerie scream of some bird in the direction of the river.

After a time, growing restless, Timothy reached over and, clicking the ignition switch to Accessory, turned on the radio. He ran the tuner along the whole length of the dial twice before he caught a glimmer of sound and zeroed in on it. It proved to be the strains of some kind of popular song, but even when he could hear the melody fairly well over the static, the words baffled him. He understood why when the music ended and an announcer's fruity voice said *"Ici Radio-Canada, CBF, Montréal."* No wonder he couldn't make it out. It was in French. Though he'd had a year of the language in school, he'd never gotten better than a C in it. It wasn't that he was dumb, exactly. It was just that he couldn't work up much enthusiasm about knowing how to say "I'm sleepy," and "It's raining," and "Where is the railroad station?" There were enough people going around saying boring and trivial stuff in English without some of them learning to say it in French, too.

He sighed, said the only French expletive he knew, *"Merde,"* and twirled the tuning knob around again. Thinking he heard a few faint words, he jiggled it delicately, trying to bring them in. When he heard the voice again, he realized it was coming from outside the car. Turning down the volume, he listened until he heard it again. "Timothy!" The voice came from the camp. "Yo! Timotheee!"

Timothy swung open the door of the Jeep and yelled back, "Whaaat?"

"Get up here!"

"What now?" he muttered to himself, and, jumping out, slammed the door shut and strode up the hill to where the tent sat.

His father had pounded six head-high stakes upright in the sandy soil and laid poles across them. Now he was trying to stretch a huge plastic tarp over the top of the frame.

"What are you making?" Timothy asked casually.

"Grab the other end of that," his father said shortly. Timothy took hold of the tarp at one corner. "Not there! In the middle!" Timothy moved down a couple of feet. "The middle! And use both hands!" The wind caught at the tarp and yanked it from Timothy's grasp. "I said grab it! Now grab it!" Finally his father anchored one corner and, pushing Timothy out of the way, proceeded to tie down the opposite corner, then the remaining ones. "There," he said, more civil now. "Our own outdoor cafe. A couple of logs for a table and one for a bench, and we'll be sitting pretty."

"Seems like a lot of trouble for just a couple of days," Timothy said.

"A couple of days? We've got more'n a week, buddy."

"Oh," said Timothy dully. "I thought—"

"What?"

"I don't know. I just thought we'd do something else for a few days."

"Like what?"

"I don't know. See some country. Stay at a motel. Take in a movie. I don't know."

"Ahh, you can do that kind of stuff at home." His father clapped a hand on Timothy's shoulder. "Let's round up some firewood and cook supper."

TWO

TIMOTHY DIDN'T SLEEP WELL that night, either—not so much because of the animal sounds, real or imagined, but because his air mattress chose some ungodly hour of the night to go flat, and he spent the rest of the time until dawn trying to find a comfortable position. He never found it. Actually, not quite until dawn, for at five-thirty his father's wrist alarm went off, and Timothy had to crawl out and walk through the same sopping grass to the river. This time when they returned they had one sizable bass which, when cleaned, just managed to whet their appetites for some more canned lunch meat fried with bread.

This day was even longer and more boring than the previous one. Even his father, once he had gotten the camp chores out of the way and patched the leaking air mattress, seemed restless. By late afternoon, Timothy was reduced to dropping crumbs and watching the ants carry them away, while his father devoted himself to digging a deep trench around the perimeter of the tent, just in case rain should suddenly decide to pour from the cloudless blue sky above them. There would be no point, however, in mentioning the total absence of rain clouds. His father would only shrug and say, "You know the Boy Scout motto."

Of course he knew it. How could he not know it, after hearing it every day for the past ten years—and twice a day when Kevin joined the local Scout troop. Being still at an age when he wanted to emulate his big brother, Timothy had joined the Cub Scouts at the same time. He stuck with it for just short of a month —until he'd picked up poison ivy on a botanical field trip.

Sighing, Timothy tossed down the last of the bread crumbs, sending the ants into a frenzy. "You know, maybe we should go into town and lay in some supplies," he suggested, secretly hoping he might pick up a paperback of some description, or at least a couple of comic books. Now he knew how an alcoholic felt when deprived of drink. "I mean," he went on, "since the fish don't seem to want to bite. I mean, we've got to eat something."

His father glanced at him reproachfully. "They'll bite. I just haven't found the right bait yet."

"Why don't you try some of that canned lunch meat?" Timothy said, wondering how far it was to the nearest Burger King. Utica, maybe?

"Besides," his father said, "it's at least twenty miles to the nearest store."

17

Timothy wobbled one of the shelter poles aimlessly. "I just thought it'd be something to do."

"Quit that. You'll tear the tarp. You want something to do? I'll give you something to do. Take the ax and go cut us a pile of firewood. It's going to be cold tonight." Timothy made a face. "What's the matter?" his father said. "I thought you wanted something to do."

"Not that. I never even used an ax before."

"Well, then, it's about time you learned how, isn't it? Besides, you could use the exercise. Look at you." He gave Timothy a whack in the gut that almost knocked the wind out of him. "Uh-huh. You see? Here." He stood up and thrust out his own stomach. "You do that to me."

"Aw, c'mon . . ."

"Go ahead. Hit me right there. Hard as you can."

"I don't want to hit you . . ."

"Go on!"

Timothy gave him a half-hearted punch.

"Oh, come on! I said hard!"

With a sigh, Timothy hauled off and gave it everything he had.

His father smiled with his mouth, but his eyes were not smiling. "See?" he said, in a tight sort of a voice. "Tough." Turning away, he picked up the ax and handed it to Timothy. "Now go do like I said. An hour of dragging in firewood and you'll be glad to sit around and do nothing for a while."

Reluctantly, Timothy took the ax. "And what if I cut my leg off?"

"Just be careful, that's all. Don't cut toward yourself."

Slowly, Timothy started out of the clearing. "Oh," his father called after him. I knew there'd be something else, Timothy thought. "And you won't need to cut down any standing timber. Just cut up the dead stuff that's already fallen." Timothy managed a few more steps before his father added, "And no little stuff. It burns too fast. Stuff as big around as your arm or bigger. Hardwood, if you can find any. You know what hardwood is? Maple or oak."

"I know." Timothy went on, swinging the ax at his side.

"And carry that thing up here, over your shoulder, or you *will* cut your leg off!"

"Yeah, yeah," Timothy grumbled, now that he was far enough away not to be heard, and laid the ax across one shoulder.

He didn't bother to look for any suitable trees until he was quite a distance from the camp, not wanting to do his cutting where his father could check up on him and criticize his awkward axmanship. For a while he only walked. After the first hundred yards or so, he took to holding the ax handle up before him to intercept the sticky spiders' webs that hung invisibly across his path, always just at face level.

Aside from these webs, which were, as far as he could tell, unoccupied, he saw almost no sign of life around him. Where were the possessors of those innumerable voices he'd heard all night long? Holed up somewhere, most likely, awaiting the evening to irritate him again. But what about the squirrels, the rabbits, the deer? The birds, even. There must be something that ran around during the day. This was the wilderness, after all. Where were the wild animals? Surely the acid rain didn't affect mammals and birds the way it did fish.

Timothy heard a rustling sound off to his left and jerked his head around, but whatever it was that had made the noise was gone now, or camouflaged so well he couldn't see it. He was pretty sure a bear would have made a more substantial racket. Probably it was just a rabbit or a chipmunk. The ranger hadn't mentioned wolves—surely it couldn't be a wolf. They ran in packs, anyway.

A chilly breath of wind hit the back of his neck, and, shivering, Timothy turned up his collar and began to scout around him for a dead tree he could chop up. Though he came across a number of them, they were either too big or too small, or else they were evergreens; his father had said to be sure and get hardwood. Finally he discovered one about four inches in diameter, leaning against another tree, and it still had some dead maple leaves clinging to it. That ought to suit his father. Timothy gripped the ax like a baseball bat—of course, he didn't grip a baseball bat right either, according to the Little League coach who had tried, several seasons back, to make Timothy into a crack right fielder like his brother. Needless to say, the whole thing hadn't been Timothy's idea, any more than the woodchopping was.

Why couldn't his father just let him be the way he was, like his mom did, instead of always trying to make him over in his own image, or in Kevin's?

Timothy gave the fallen tree a half-hearted chop. The ax bounced off, leaving little more than a scar on the bark. Kevin would know how to handle an ax. He'd probably have had the whole tree cut up and carried back to camp by now. Timothy swung the ax harder. After about fifty blows, he managed to worry the wood in two, and he sat down, winded. This was going to be even more work than he had thought. Discouraged, he looked around for something a little more manageable. As big around as his arm, his father had said. Whose arm—his or his father's?

Spotting a tangle of fallen limbs not far off, Timothy got to his feet and, trudging over, began to pull at some of the larger ones. These were so long dead that they broke into pieces with a single stroke of the ax. This was more like it. Timothy pulled off the down-filled vest he had been wearing and began to attack the wood determinedly. Before long, he had built up a sizable pile of chunks and, puffing, he sat down to rest again.

Only now did he notice how late it was getting. He could no longer see the sun glinting through the treetops; it must have sunk close to the horizon. When the heat he had worked up swinging the ax began to dissipate, the sweat along his spine grew cold and clammy. It was time he started back. He slipped on the vest and, kneeling, stacked as many of the wood chunks as he could hold between his chest and one arm.

As an afterthought, he picked up the ax and stuck it under his other arm. If he left it there, even temporarily, his father was sure to make a big hairy deal out of it. He turned to leave. There was only one problem —he wasn't quite sure in which direction the camp lay.

Frowning, he scanned the woods around him. He spotted a dead tree leaning against a live one some distance away and headed for it, feeling more confident. But when he reached the spot, he could find no sign of all the chopping he had done earlier—this was obviously not the same tree. "Well, now, come on," he said aloud, irritably.

Scratching his head, he took another look around, located another leaning dead tree, and made for it. He was beginning to feel the weight of the armload of wood now, and he pitched about a third of it, telling himself he would retrieve it later. The second dead tree, when he reached it, was as devoid of ax marks as the first one. "Crap," he muttered, and tossed the remainder of his woodpile to the ground. "This is ridiculous." The forest was growing dusky now, and he could no longer see clearly for any distance. Nor could he spot any more leaning trees.

He felt a surge of nausea-like panic in the pit of his stomach, and he opened his mouth to yell for help. Then he caught himself and shook his head. "No," he muttered under his breath. "I'm not going to give him the satisfaction. Now come on," he went on, whispering to himself. "You can't be far from camp. All you have to do is, you walk in a big circle, and you're bound to come across it, or else the logging road. Okay. Okay. Let's see." He glanced around again and then, taking a deep breath, stepped away from the tree. It felt like stepping into a void, though of course the tree he had been standing next to was no real landmark at all, only a place he thought he had been. Still, it was a definite place, and now he was no place in particular.

An owl hooted, sounding almost on top of him, and he started, and picked up his pace. In the growing dusk, the trees were like a maze or an obstacle course, and though he tried hard to follow the circumference of his imaginary circle, there was always some brush or a fallen tree to detour around, so that he began to lose all track of his direction.

Soon it was quite dark, and the sick, desperate feeling had begun to grip him again, when he stumbled into a clear space and realized that he had found the old logging road. For a moment he stood there, panting and grinning in relief, until it dawned on him that he still didn't know in which direction to follow the road. "Surely it's that way," he told himself, softly, pointing to his right. "Yeah, sure, it's got to be. Anyway, if I don't come across it soon, all I have to do is turn around and go back the other way. Simple, right? Okay."

Hefting the ax, he started off at a trot, promptly turned his ankle in one of the overgrown ruts, and slowed down to a limping walk. He expected at any minute to see the glow of a campfire ahead of him, and

23

he began to wonder what his father was going to have to say about his absence. Undoubtedly he'd be disgusted. "How can anybody get lost cutting *firewood*, for crying out loud? What were you, about a hundred yards from camp? And to top it off, I notice you didn't even bring back the firewood!" Something along those lines. Well, at least he hadn't been dumb enough to call for help. At least he'd found his way out on his own. If his father had had to tramp around through the woods trying to find him, he'd really have been ticked off.

Timothy began to notice, despite the fact that he could hardly see, that the road was getting more and more weed-choked and narrow as he went along. In some places there were even a few good-sized bushes flourishing between the wheel ruts, and he stumbled into most of them. He hadn't remembered the road being quite so wild on their trip into camp, but then everything seemed different at night. Still, if the going got any more rough, it might indicate he had chosen the wrong direction after all. For the time being, he decided to keep on the way he was headed.

It wasn't long before it became obvious that there was no camp ahead, or much of anything else, for he ran directly into a thicket of bushes that stood nearly as tall as he did—which, admittedly, was not very tall. Sumac, he guessed, from the feel of the hairy clumps of berries at the ends of the branches. He shrank back. He seemed to recall from some unknown source that sumac was supposed to be poison.

24

Well, obviously bushes that size had not grown there overnight. Still, it was no tragedy, he told himself, while he tried to ignore the queasy feeling of fear that butted insistently at his stomach. A slight miscalculation, that was all. All he had to do was turn around and trek back the other way. With a sigh, he did an about-face and started walking again. As boring as the camp was and as uncomfortable as he felt in the tiny tent, they were going to seem almost like home when he finally got back.

Above the sound of his harsh breathing and his boots scuffling along the path, Timothy heard a faint cry. "Probably just another owl," he muttered, but he walked more softly and listened more intently anyway. The sound came again, from far off. Timothy halted and cupped one ear with his hand. Nothing—only the whisper of the fretful breeze. Then, just as he was about to go on, he heard it again, carried on the wind—his father's voice, calling something indistinguishable.

"Yeah!" Timothy shouted. "Yeah! I'm coming!" He plunged into the brush alongside the road, making for the source of the sound. "I'm coming!" he hollered again as he felt his way along.

He had run no more than fifty yards when his foot struck some projecting root or rock, and he crashed headlong to the ground. For a second he lay doubled up there in agony, gasping to regain the wind that had been knocked out of him. When finally his stunned diaphragm recovered and he began to breathe again, he sat up, groaning and rubbing the left side of his rib cage, where he had struck a stone. "Oh, man," he complained weakly, almost in tears. "What a dumbbell. What a dumb klutz."

As he sat there trying to collect himself, he heard the voice calling again, even fainter now. "I'm here!" he yelled, in a broken voice that he knew would never be heard. It wasn't until he tried to rise that he realized the real extent of the damage the fall had done. The first thing he noticed was that his glasses were no longer on his face. The second thing was the sudden, searing pain in his right knee when he tried to stand. With a cry, he collapsed on the ground again, almost in a faint.

When his brain stopped whirling, he sat up slowly and gingerly explored the injured leg with his fingers. He touched a long, ragged tear in his jeans; the fabric all around it was soaked. At first he thought he had tumbled into a puddle, but then he felt more wetness oozing onto his hand. "Holy cow," he murmured. "It's my blood." He felt suddenly faint again and lay back in the weeds, breathing rapidly and hoarsely. After a moment, his mind cleared enough for him to recognize the important fact that if he didn't somehow stop the flow of bood, and soon, when his father finally found him, he'd find nothing but a cold corpse.

THREE

WITH HIS TEETH CLENCHED against the pain, Timothy sat up again, more slowly still. He got no further than propping himself up on one arm before another surge of dizziness numbed his mind, and he had to slump back into a prone position. The whole thing was like one of those awful dreams that occur on the threshold of waking, where you feel that something menacing is about to happen but you can't quite muster the energy to rise out of bed and prevent it.

He lay still a few minutes, panting and sweating profusely in spite of the cold ground beneath him, until the pain became more immediate than the dizziness. Hearing some noise nearby, he held his breath, trying to listen past the pounding of his own pulse in his ears. Maybe it was his father calling, on his way to this very spot.

But there was no sound. Most likely he had heard only some night creature rustling about—a raccoon on its way to the river, or a possum scrounging for whatever it was possums ate. No use calling out, then. You couldn't count on possums or raccoons to know much about first aid. If he was going to get out of this thing, he was going to have to do it by himself. The trouble was, he'd never been any good in a crisis. He just wasn't the sort who always knew what to do. His mind didn't work that way—it took him some time to figure out a situation. But how much time did he have? How long did it take to bleed to death? Half an hour? How long had he lain here already? He had no idea.

He prodded his brain. Surely out of all the books he had read, he must have come across something that addressed itself to this particular situation. What was that John Steinbeck story where the kid got shot? He'd put something—cobwebs!—on the wound. Well, that was a big help. He'd walked through a zillion spider webs earlier in the day—where were they when he needed them? Besides, as he recalled, the kid in the story had died.

So, what was he supposed to do? Make a tourniquet? No, he was pretty sure that was only for when you cut an artery, and it didn't seem likely that he'd cut an artery, or he'd probably be dead by now.

Apply pressure to the wound, then? With what? He patted his pockets and, feeling a lump in one, dug down and came up with the handkerchief his mother had insisted he take along because he was sure to need it. Probably this wasn't what she'd had in mind.

Afraid to sit up again, Timothy took hold of his

injured leg with both hands and, grunting with the pain and effort, lifted it so that it was propped up in the air atop his bent left leg. He yanked at the rip in his pants leg to open it wider and, biting his lip, pressed the bundled handkerchief to the wound. The touch of it made him wince and cry out.

He held it there only a moment before he felt the cloth growing wet under his fingertips. He must be bleeding pretty hard. How long did it take the pressure method to work, anyway? And what did you do if it didn't? He pressed harder.

It occurred to him now to wonder how he could have managed to hurt himself so badly just tripping over a rock. At first he decided he must have struck another stone, a sharp-edged one, with his knee. Then he remembered the ax. Of course. He'd been swinging it at his side as he ran. Oh, great. He'd never hear the last of that. "I *told* you to carry it over your shoulder! And how many times have I said to never run with a tool in your hand?" Maybe he'd be better off just to lie here and bleed to death. Then they'd be sorry. He'd told his father he didn't want to cut wood in the first place. Heck, he'd never even wanted to come to the Adirondacks in the place before that. He knew something would go wrong. Something always did. If he'd had his way, he'd be lying in bed at home reading a book right now, instead of lying here in the woods, bleeding to death. Better to read than bleed. Better read than dead. Funny, he felt almost drunk, or what he imagined being drunk would feel like—lightheaded, a faint buzzing in his ears, a tingling in the crooks of his arms. The pain had even subsided a little. Maybe this was what it felt like to die, just a sort of fading awareness, like in the Jack London story where the man couldn't build a fire and lay down in a snowdrift and went to sleep.

Gradually, without his having noticed, his injured leg had begun to slip off its perch on his good one, and now it flopped to the ground, sending a jolt of pain through him. Timothy let out a yell and clutched at it. Some creature crashed off through the brush, startled by his outcry. What kind of creature? A deer? A bear? Were bears like sharks, attracted by the smell of blood?

Timothy shuddered violently, as much from the cold, which was beginning to seep into him, as from the thought of bears. This was not a good place to spend the hours until daylight, when his father would surely come to find him. Hoisting himself up carefully onto one elbow, he lifted the handkerchief from the wound. After a moment, he touched his fingers to the flesh. There was still a bit of wetness there, but not a regular flow of blood like before. So far so good.

What he needed now was a more durable bandage. He searched his pants pockets again and came up with the folding knife-fork-spoon combination he'd picked out at the outdoor store—his sole contribution to their outfit of wilderness gear. He had wanted to get a collapsible drinking cup, too, but his father had drawn the line at that.

Timothy unfolded the knife blade and, after considering for a minute, pulled out his shirttail. Sawing through the front edge of the fabric with the dull blade, he ripped off a strip about two or three inches wide all the way around the tail of the shirt. When he had returned the knife to his pocket, he leaned forward and, groaning, propped his injured leg up over the good one again. Then he wrapped the shirttail bandage around the knee, as tightly as he could stand it. When he was finished, he collapsed again, exhausted.

Obviously he was not going anywhere for quite a while. If he couldn't even sit up for more than two minutes at a time, he surely wasn't about to get up and go trudging through the woods. It looked like he would be spending the night here after all. There had been no more calls from his father—presuming it really was his father, and not some animal cleverly imitating him—for quite some time, so he'd better not count on being rescued until morning.

So, how did a person go about preparing to spend the night in the woods? In the books he'd read, it seemed like they always laid themselves a bed of spruce boughs and then lit themselves a fire and sat around roasting rabbits on a stick. It sounded good, but unfortunately he could neither see nor get around to gather spruce boughs—he wasn't even sure there were any spruce trees in the vicinity—he had no way of lighting a fire, and the only thing he had to kill a rabbit with, even if one should happen by, was a folding knife-fork-spoon combination. The stick he might be able to manage.

It looked like about the best he could do was to try and locate the ax and his glasses, and maybe drag himself into the shelter of a tree, where at least he'd have his back to something if a bear or a lynx or a wolverine came around.

The ax ought to be easy enough to find, since he'd obviously landed right on top of it. He ran both hands along the ground on either side of him and, finding nothing but rocks and weeds, wriggled around in a half-circle to explore some more. After picking up two sticks by mistake, he finally touched the smooth wood of the ax handle and drew it to him.

The glasses were going to be tougher to put his hands on. Better to wait for daylight. Holding the ax across his lap, he sat up and looked around, squinting into the dark. The night was clear enough to make the outlines of trees visible against the dark violet sky. There seemed to be a sizable evergreen of some description off to his right. Using his arms and his one good leg, he painfully scooted his body in that direction.

On the very first scoot, his rear end settled onto something hard, and he heard a muffled snap. He knew at once what had happened. The good news was that he had found his glasses; the bad news was that he had simultaneously ruined them. Sighing with the resignation of someone all too used to proving Murphy's Law —anything that can go wrong, will—Timothy leaned to one side and retrieved the glasses. As far as he could determine with his sense of touch, the lenses were still intact, but he had snapped the nose piece neatly in two. Disgusted, he tucked the halves into his shirt pocket and headed for the tree again.

This time he actually advanced several yards without any mishap, at which point he set his left hand in a patch of thistles. Growling unformed curses and shaking his stinging palm vigorously, he went on, using only one hand and one leg.

By the time he felt the prickly branches of the evergreen poking his head, his strength was drained utterly again, and he had to lie back on the ground to recuperate. The many years' worth of dry fallen needles made a sort of circular carpet at the base of the tree, insulating him a little from the cold hard dirt. If he only had something to put over himself by way of a blanket, it would be almost bearable. He wouldn't even kick now if somebody offered him that stupid, suffocating mummy bag and the leaky air mattress. He tried not to even think about the foam mattress and clean sheets and down comforter in his room at home.

What did the pioneers use for blankets? Buffalo robes, probably. Or rabbit skin robes, maybe, made out of all those rabbits they always ate? Timothy sucked reflectively on one of his thistle-pierced fingers. There had to be some way to keep warm. If you could make a bed out of evergreen boughs, maybe they'd work for covers, too. It was worth a try.

Fishing out the knife-fork-spoon combination, he reached over his head and, grunting softly to himself, began to whittle away at the branches of the tree. Though they hung very close to the ground, it was hard work cutting through them with the cheap knife blade. Before long, despite the chill in the air, he was sweating from the effort. Well, if nothing else, he could cut branches all night to keep warm.

It seemed for a while as if it might take all night to gather a big enough pile, but eventually, after stopping for several lengthy rest periods, he decided that either he had enough or he would just go ahead and freeze to death. Setting the ax against the tree trunk within easy reach, in case of unwanted visitors from the animal kingdom, he placed the boughs over himself, one by one, as meticulously as a person decorating a Christmas tree. Except this was more a case of a Christmas tree decorating a person. The needles tickled his chin and prickled his bare leg through the rip in his jeans, but otherwise they made a comfortable enough blanket.

Sighing wearily, he closed his eyes. If it weren't for the throbbing in his leg, and the rock jabbing at his spine, and the annoying pain of his thistle-ravaged hand, he might even be able to drop off to sleep for a while.

Some sound made him open his eyes again. He lay there, listening, until he heard it repeated. Nothing alarming, just a bird singing. A bird singing in the middle of the night? But then it seemed it wasn't really the middle of the night, for there was a washed-out gray tint to the sky now. So he must have drifted off after all, and it was getting on toward dawn. He lay flexing his stiff joints and twisting his aching neck from side to side until the sky grew light enough for him to see his surroundings.

It was a desolate spot he had chosen to spend the night in—well, not chosen, exactly. It could not even be called primitively awesome. The trees were mostly scrubby little affairs, three or four feet high, growing so close together that their branches interlocked like hedges. Some sort of gray moss or lichen coated their trunks, like icing on a cake.

Cake. His stomach responded violently to the thought. This was probably the longest he had gone without food since the time he broke the stereo and his father sent him to bed without supper. And even then his mom had sneaked a piece of cherry pie and a glass of milk up to him. Pie. Milk. His mouth and tongue felt like blotting paper. How long was it since he'd had a drink? Yesterday about noon? He'd lost all that blood, too. What with the cold and the lack of liquids, if his father didn't get here pretty soon, he was going to be a freeze-dried lump, like the Swiss steak trail dinners they'd brought along.

If he could just move around a little, he might work some of the chill out. Creakily, he raised himself up to a sitting position and dug the halves of his glasses out of his shirt pocket. As he had thought, the lenses were okay, though one hinge was a little on the crooked side. Brushing away his evergreen blanket, he bent over and examined his injured knee through one half of the glasses, held up like a lorgnette.

The knee looked bad with all the dried blood caked on it, but it didn't really hurt all that much any more —no more than, say, having a bad cavity poked by the dentist. Probably it should have a fresh bandage, but he was fresh out. Besides, he'd be back in camp soon, and his father would know what to do with it. Now that he thought about it, maybe he should actually be grateful for the wound, the way soldiers in a war were some-times—it wasn't so serious that he'd be crippled or anything, but bad enough to get him sent home early.

Of course, he'd have to listen to his father's griping about the whole thing, but then he was more or less accustomed to that. His father would find something to gripe about even if they stayed.

Probably he was griping even now, as he gulped down a cup of coffee before starting out to look for his incompetent son, who had done him out of a whole morning's fishing. Pretty soon he would come tramping through the bushes, having followed Timothy's trail the way he had followed that wounded deer he liked to tell about. Only every time he told the story, the dis-tance he'd had to trail the deer got longer and longer —it was up to something like ten miles at last count. If his father could track a canny deer, he should have no trouble at all following Timothy's careless wake.

One thing that puzzled Timothy, though, was why the old man hadn't thought to just lay on the car horn a few times to give him a direction, give him a chance to find his own way back. He had no way of knowing, after all, that Timothy couldn't walk. It only made sense to give some kind of signal—that's what they did when somebody was lost in all the books he'd read.

Then, for the first time, he had the chilling thought

that maybe his father wasn't completely in command of the situation after all, that maybe he didn't always know just what to do. Maybe he'd gone looking for Timothy and got lost himself. Naahhh. Timothy shrugged and shook his head. Not *his* father. Knowing him, he was more liable to just get disgusted enough to pack up and drive off, leaving Timothy to his fate.

A sudden shiver went through Timothy's frame. He'd meant that to be an exaggeration, but somehow there was enough truth in it to make it seem almost possible. After all, his father had left him stranded downtown at the movie theater that time when Timothy spent his bus fare on popcorn and candy—it would teach him a valuable lesson, his father had said on the phone; if he wanted to get home, he could walk. Well, his mother had finally broken down and come for him that time, and anyway, even if he'd had to walk it, it would have been only a matter of a couple of miles. Here it was twenty or thirty miles just to the nearest town, and Timothy hadn't the vaguest idea in what direction it lay.

But he was just thinking stupid thoughts. His father wasn't *that* mean. Most likely the reason he didn't signal was that he just didn't trust Timothy to follow his own ears. Probably he was right. His ears, thanks to frequent infections as a child, were not a whole lot better than his eyes.

Thinking he heard a distant call, he held his breath and listened. Only another bird. He tried a few tentative halloos of his own but got no response, except that the birds stopped singing temporarily. Sighing, he lay back to await his rescue.

His muscles and joints ached so much—more than the leg, really—that before long he was finding it difficult to lie still. What he needed was to drag himself into a less shaded spot and soak up some warmth from the sun, which was beginning to show itself now through the treetops. Maybe if he used the ax as a sort of crutch or cane, he could hobble into a clearing. It would be a lot easier for his father to spot him, too, if he was out in the open.

Grunting, Timothy clambered out slowly from under the branches of the tree and, warily turning the blade of the ax away from him, used the tool to help himself into a standing position. The blood rushing down into his bad knee set it throbbing, and he grimaced and almost had to sit down again. But as he stood there a moment, leaning his weight on the ax handle, the pain gradually became less insistent.

He blew out his breath wearily and took a small exploratory step forward. A journey of a thousand miles begins with a single step, they said. Well, hopefully it wasn't a thousand miles to the nearest clearing.

As a matter of fact, it wasn't far at all. Seeing a sunny patch of ground some distance off, he hobbled toward it. After stopping only once to rest, he reached the spot, to find a sizable expanse of sumac and briers so thick as to discourage any aspiring trees. He sat down on a fallen, rotting log whose farthest reaches were swallowed by the tangled growth, then stretched his injured leg out before him. Slipping off his vest, he closed his eyes and let the sun bake his aching muscles as it burned the dew off the grass.

The warmth soon made him drowsy, and several times he found himself jerking erect and awake, having slumped forward almost to the point of falling off the log. In this dreamlike state, he began to imagine things: He heard his father calling out, and he could hear the words now, but they were not what he expected—he was not crying, "Timothy, where are you?" but "Timothy, help! I'm lost!" Timothy started and looked around vaguely for a moment, then slowly drifted off again. This time it seemed to him that the ax, which he had leaned against the log, was falling; its blade landed on his leg, cutting him, and though he pushed it away as hard as he could, somehow it fell again and then again, hacking at him almost deliberately. He woke with a gasp.

The ax stood where he had left it. All the same, he reached over and, taking hold of it firmly, leaned over backward to lay it on the ground on the far side of the log. Almost at once he wished he hadn't, for a sudden and disconcerting crashing, crunching racket erupted from somewhere in the mass of brush before him. He shook his head sharply, thinking he might be dreaming again. Convinced that he wasn't, Timothy scanned the tangle anxiously, looking for the source of the noise, which continued unabated. It was even augmented now by a series of hoarse, almost human grunts.

Timothy swallowed hard and called out, hesitantly and hopefully, "Dad?"

FOUR

THE NOISE STOPPED ABRUPTLY. Timothy's heartbeat pounded in his ears in the sudden silence. A bird piped up somewhere in the woods. A fly droned around his face, and he tossed his head slightly, almost afraid to move. "Dad?" he called again, in a strained voice.

With an abruptness that made him jump, the noise resumed. Only now it seemed to be moving away from rather than toward him, and at a much quicker pace. Timothy dragged himself to his feet just in time to catch a glimpse of a black, lumbering shape disappearing among the trees on the opposite side of the clearing.

Timothy shook his head again, dazed. "Oh, man!" he breathed. "I don't believe it! A bear!" It had to be. There was nothing else that big in the woods, except maybe deer, and he was pretty sure they didn't come in black. If he had been able to climb a tree, or even run away, he would have done so. As it was, he had to content himself with crouching down with his back pressed against the fallen tree, gripping the ax tightly, listening fearfully all ears for the bear's return.

He kept his eyes busy, too. This time the beast might decide to come from some entirely new direction, so as to confound him. He remembered reading somewhere that bears were very intelligent and crafty animals— not to mention bad-tempered and brutal—especially protective mother bears. He hadn't seen any sign of cubs, but that didn't mean there weren't a couple around which might sniff him out, curious, and bring down their mother's wrath on him.

His leg began to throb unmercifully, due to the awkwardness of his position. Summoning up his courage, Timothy went so far as to shift his body around a few inches to make himself a little more comfortable. For the incessant pain in his empty stomach, he could do nothing. Did people eat bear meat? More to the point, did bears eat people meat?

When nearly an hour had passed by his watch, which had somehow survived all his mishaps, and there was no surprise attack and no noise more threatening than an eagle's cry overhead, he raised himself cautiously onto the log again. As he gazed out over the thicket, it occurred to him for the first time to wonder why the bear had been rummaging through it so energetically. Could it have been foraging for food? If so, what kind of food?

Throwing a little of his caution, at least, to the winds, he limped eagerly over to the edge of the tangle.

Sure enough, mixed in with the bare brambles were some low bushes clustered with small but abundant blue berries. He picked one and tasted it warily. Though it was a bit on the seedy side, it had the familiar flavor of blueberries. Timothy began to pluck the tiny berries and devour them as fast as he could with one hand, while supporting himself with the other on the handle of the ax. He was not, however, so unwary as to forget that he was not the only berry-loving animal in the vicinity. As he ate, he glanced around continually and nervously in every direction, like a bird at a feeder.

When he had eaten all he could hold and his picking hand was as stained as the bandage around his knee, he limped back to the log and, for a long time, just sat there with the ax across his knees, watching for his father, or the bear, whichever came first. After an hour or so, he began to feel the hardness of the wood under him and, taking up his down vest, he folded it for a cushion. As he sat on it, he felt some object pressing against him. Unfolding the vest again, he searched the pockets and, to his surprise, he drew out a thin paper-back book. "I'll be darned," he said softly, delightedly. It was a well-worn copy of *Lord of the Flies* he had been reading last winter and had been unable to find since then. Obviously he had been carrying it around with him and, when warm weather came, had shut the book, along with the vest, away in his clothes closet until a few days ago, when his mother had made him dig it out for the camping trip.

Timothy patted the book as he would have an old friend—if he'd had any old friends. When they lived in Pennsylvania he had friends—at least a couple, the kids he had grown up with. But then, of course, when he was ten they picked up and moved to Elmira, where his father had a job offer. It had worked out okay for his father—he owned the company now. Timothy hadn't made out so well. He wasn't like Kevin, who made friends as easily as he made goals or base hits— as easily as he did everything. Of course, the friends Timothy did have were of a much higher caliber. Who did Kevin know that was anywhere near as good company as Mark Twain or Sherlock Holmes?

Timothy riffled through the pages of the book and then, refolding the vest-cushion, settled down again and opened to page one. Now, if he only had a case of soda and a couple of bags of chips, this business of being lost wouldn't be so bad.

He found it difficult, though, to keep his mind on the book. At every sound—and the woods seemed filled with them—he glanced up anxiously. In spite of—or perhaps because of—the berry feast, his stomach was complaining. His injured knee itched and throbbed unmercifully.

After only a few pages, he carefully set the book down next to him and, propping the bad leg up on a limb of the tree, gingerly unwrapped the stiff shirttail bandage. When he reached the end of it, he found it was stuck to the wound with dried blood. Working up the best mouthful of saliva he could manage in view of his lack of water, he spit on the knee repeatedly until he had it wet enough to pull free with only a moderate amount of agony. With a little more spit, he washed away some of the blood around the wound so he could get a better idea of how bad it really was.

It was bad enough to qualify as the worst wound he'd ever had—but then he'd always been careful, if clumsy, as a child. The ax blade had sliced loose a flap of skin maybe four or five inches long just above and to one side of his kneecap. Fortunately the makeshift bandage had held the flap closed tightly enough so it was already beginning to heal in place. If he could just keep from moving the knee for a while, it might do all right.

He held up the bloodstained bandage. His mother would have conniptions if she saw that. Surprisingly, he himself, who had nearly lost his lunch once over a dissected frog in biology lab, hardly felt squeamish looking at it. After all, anybody who could sustain a major flesh wound and still have the presence of mind to fashion a bandage and stop the bleeding was not so faint of heart as some people thought. He was almost of a mind to redo the knee in the bloody wrapping, just to impress everyone when he was found. A sort of Red Badge of Courage. However, he decided against it; it would be very unsanitary. Besides, the cut itched less with the bandage off. He left it uncovered. Maybe the sunshine would do it some good, too. Picking up *Lord of the Flies,* he started to read again.

He still couldn't concentrate on the words. It was like trying to read in a dentist's office, all the while wondering if you were going to get off easy or have to suffer. Only in this case it wasn't his teeth at stake—it was his life. What was keeping his father? What if he wasn't able to find him for some reason? Already it was past noon. How long should he sit here waiting? Until the bear came back? Until he died of thirst? If he had to stay another night in the woods, he'd do well to find some spot with a supply of water nearby—and no bears.

He decided to wait a few more hours where he was and then, if he wasn't found . . . but surely he would be found. If his father couldn't locate him, he'd just drive back to the ranger station—it was only fifteen or twenty miles at the most—and get help: a search party, maybe even helicopters. He'd be found.

But the afternoon came and went, and Timothy heard no calls or rifle shots, and saw no plane or chopper cross the sky. What was taking them so long? Surely his father had gotten worried enough by now to return to the ranger station and alert them. Or maybe he hadn't. His father had never been the type to ask anyone else for help. That was too much like giving up, admitting defeat. Knowing him, he'd probably keep searching until he saw there was no chance of finding his son on his own. Of course, by that time his son might well be dehydrated bear food.

No. No, that wasn't going to happen. If his father could be stubborn, then so could Timothy. Somehow he was going to hang on until he was rescued, whether it was his father who found him or a search party consisting of the entire ranger force and the population of North Wilmurt. Whether it was today or a week from today. Of course, he would prefer that it not be a week. But it didn't really look like it was going to be today, either. His watch said five o'clock—that meant maybe three hours of daylight left. If he was going to find a decent spot to spend the night, he'd better get hopping—literally.

First he had to bind up the wound again. By the time he cut a second strip from his shirttail, it was too short to tuck into his pants any more. It had been practically a brand-new shirt, too. His mom was going to kill him when he got home.

Wrapping the knee tightly, he took up his vest and his ax-cane and, hobbling over to the thicket, stuffed himself again. It might be a while before he came across another berry patch. If he only had something in which he could carry a few with him, a basket or . . .

Wait a minute. The Indian tribes all made baskets, didn't they? Out of what? Reeds? Birch bark? He glanced around him. There were several white birches not far off, at the edge of the clearing. Well, he had nothing better to do except read, and it might be a good idea to ration that, since he was undoubtedly a long way from the nearest library.

The hardest part was getting to the trees. Once he made his painful way to them, it was a fairly easy matter to chop a large square out of the bark and, pushing the edge of the ax blade under one edge, peel it loose. He had made small boxes out of construction paper at home several times, and he made something similar, only narrower and deeper, out of the bark square, turning up the edges and pinning the corners together with twigs pushed through like rivets.

When he was finished, he held up and examined his handiwork. A little flimsy, maybe, but not bad for a first try. Probably the Indians sewed theirs together with spruce roots, or deer sinew, or some such thing, but his would do. Back to the berry bushes. By the time he had the basket full, he desperately needed a rest, but he made it a short one. The sun was dropping close to the treetops already.

If he was going to have to move on, his first instinct was to go back the way he had come. But what good would that do? He hadn't known where he was when he was there, either. Besides, that direction lay slightly uphill, and if he wanted to find water, it was only logical to go downhill—not to mention the fact that it was a whole lot easier to walk down a slope than up. Anyway, when you had no idea which way civilization lay, one direction was as good as another.

He knew there were ways of determining which way north and south lay—there was something about making a line halfway between the hour hand of your watch and the numeral twelve. Presumably that didn't apply, though, if your watch, like his, had a digital face. Not that it would do him any good anyway, since he had no idea toward which compass point he went when he left camp, or anytime thereafter.

He recalled reading a story once in which a man who was hopelessly lost managed to save himself by following the course of creeks and rivers, always heading downstream, until he came upon a settlement. Of course, the story took place in the jungle, and the village turned out to be occupied by savage headhunters. Still, theoretically it sounded like a good idea. Downhill it was, then.

Timothy forced himself to his weary feet again and, lifting his bulging basket carefully, he began to circle the berry thicket. When he got almost to the far side, it occurred to him that he had left behind something every bit as indispensable as the ax—the book. It still lay on the fallen tree trunk. For just a moment he hesitated, looking over the considerable distance he had come, and then with a heavy sigh he laid the berries and the vest in the grass and hobbled back to fetch the book.

When he finally reached the far side of the bramble patch, he saw the swath cut in it by the fleeing bear. It looked as though a tank had plowed through the tangle, flattening a yard-wide path. Whistling under his breath, Timothy steered clear of the spot. He was in no condition to try and outrun an animal with four good legs to his one.

As he entered the woods, he saw what he took to be another bear sign. On a large tree trunk, just above the level of his head, there was a whitish patch where the bark had been raked away in gashes an inch deep. If a set of claws could do that much damage to a tree trunk, think what they would do to paltry human flesh. Shuddering, Timothy hurried on.

Until he came across the blaze and the trampled briers, he had almost been inclined to think that he had imagined seeing the bear, or dreamed it. The woods seemed otherwise so entirely devoid of life, except for the occasional two cents' worth put in by some bird. You could see more wildlife than this at his aunt's house in suburban Pittsburgh, where rabbits turned up in threes and fours to nibble at her well-kept back yard, and occasionally a groundhog came around to check things out. Several times his aunt said she had even spotted deer on the hillside behind the house.

So, if the forest here was so dead, and the lakes dying, why did people go on so about preserving the park in its "natural state"? If nothing else was willing or able to live here, they might just as well cut down the trees and saw them up into lumber and build houses for people to live in.

If this had been a housing development instead of a forest, he wouldn't have gotten lost. All he'd have had to do was remember the street names and, if worst came to worst, it would be easy to ask someone for help. Of course, if this were all houses and streets and yards, he wouldn't have been out cutting wood, either, because there wouldn't be any; they wouldn't even have camped here. In fact, his father never would have brought him here in the first place.

If people insisted on leaving all this wilderness sitting around, the least they could do was put in a network of roads and trails, with signs every so often to tell you where you were and where you were going, and maybe some little shelters here and there, with vending machines or something.

Even as he planned these practical improvements in his mind, Timothy found to his surprise that he had, indeed, stumbled onto some sort of path through the trees. He stopped and peered along it. It wasn't very wide or well-marked, but it was a definite trail; the moss and needles and ferns that blanketed the rest of the forest floor hung back here, leaving a strip a foot or two wide of bare dirt and wiry, trampled weeds. Someone or something had walked here repeatedly, and probably recently, if Timothy was any judge . . . which, unfortunately, he was not. Still, it was something he could easily follow, a direction in which to go. After all, if it *was* a trail, it had to lead somewhere, right? Even if it only led to a trapper's cabin or an old logging camp, it was better than being nowhere, which was where he was now.

Feeling a bit more optimistic, Timothy allowed himself a short rest. He sat down on a mossy rock and ate a few of his berries. Though the trees blocked his view of the sun's position, he guessed that dusk couldn't be far off. He checked his watch. Five-twenty.

Five-twenty? That didn't make sense. The last time he checked, it had said five o'clock, and that was hours ago. He looked closer. The dots that flashed the seconds weren't flashing. Great. He must have knocked it against something when he was cutting the birch bark. Well, when it came right down to it, it didn't much matter anyway. It would get dark when it got dark, no matter what his watch said.

Though he knew there was no sense in wearing the watch any longer, something—he wasn't sure just what—kept him from pitching it. It might have been some bit of reluctance to impose it on the wild scenery around him, or it may just have been that it gave him a certain sense of security, that throwing it away would be like casting off one more small link with civilization.

Now that there was no way of telling when dusk would come on, Timothy felt the need to hurry. He got wearily to his feet and hobbled on, keeping to the trail now. Though there were no markers or blazes, it was easy enough to follow—until it split suddenly. Then he had to make the difficult decision of which fork to take. Unlike Robert Frost in the poem, he took the one that looked to him to be more traveled, though it was really more or less arbitrary.

Even with no obstacles blocking his path, he found the going tough. The only way to avoid bending his bad leg was to thrust it out to one side, and as a consequence, he repeatedly bumped either the leg or his left side against the trees between which the path weaved. Before long, he noticed a red spot on the shirttail bandage, one too large and too round to be part of the plaid pattern of the cloth. "Aw, no," he wailed. "It broke open again."

A few more steps and he found a suitable rock and plunked himself down on it, only to discover to his dismay that the wound wasn't the only thing that had broken open—his pseudo-Indian birch-bark basket had sprung a leak, and no more than a cup or two of berries remained in the bottom. Timothy groaned and clapped a hand to his forehead. He had been carrying the basket under his arm and had probably squeezed it too hard one of the times when he had knocked up against a tree. Desolately, he looked up the trail. Well, if he should ever need to retrace his steps the way he had come, it would be a real cinch, for there was an unmistakable string of blueberries winding Hansel-and-Gretel-like through the woods.

"I don't believe it," he said. "Wrong-Way Tim has done it again." Wrong-Way Tim. Funny he should dredge that up after all this time. It had been his nickname for a year or so following the touchdown he made for the opposing team in a game of touch football. Nobody had wanted him to play in the first place, except Kevin, who for once, had stood up for him; and then Timothy had let him down by pulling a stunt like that. Since he always seemed to be doing everything wrong, the name had stuck. It had finally given way to other nicknames, but when word got around at school about how he'd gotten himself lost, it might enjoy a revival.

Maybe it would be better if they never did find him. Maybe he could just stay here and be a hermit and live on roots and berries. Of course, he'd still have to compete with the bear. There was always somebody to contend with, it seemed, even in the woods.

As he sat there, trying to figure out what to do next, he became gradually aware of a faint sound in the distance that he hadn't noticed before, a sound like several voices chatting in unison, incessantly and incoherently, rather the way *The Tonight Show* sounded when heard through an open window in a house far down the block.

Timothy almost shouted. So the trail did lead someplace! Jumping up, he grabbed his few belongings and limped furiously ahead, careless of the wounded leg now that salvation was at hand.

FIVE

WHEN HE HAD GONE only a little way, the trail grew abruptly steeper, so that he was hard put to keep his balance. Since the berry basket only hampered him, he tossed it and its measly contents aside.

Now the ground dropped off even more steeply, and the trail, instead of dropping with it, cut across the contour of the slope, switching back now and again to make the descent less steep. Soon Timothy was exhausted, and he was forced to rest on a ledge of thick moss. When his breathing and heartbeat subsided, he listened again for the voices. Only now that he was closer, the voices had metamorphosed, like a mirage of the ears, into something more prosaic: the nattering, chuckling sound of a stream.

Timothy shook his head and sighed heavily. He should have known. Well, at least he had made a little quick progress. Besides, he had been looking for water, so it was hardly a total loss. The only thing was, he wished he hadn't pitched the berries.

More slowly this time, he rose and made his way on down the trail. Before long he could see the creek below him. There was no bridge, no house, no sign of human life—not even a continuation of the trail; it stopped at the water's edge. He stopped there as well, on a sandy bit of riverbank that was perforated by many dozens of small, sharp hoofprints. The path he had been following so eagerly and trustingly was no man-made thoroughfare, after all—only an ancient trace worn by deer on their way to a watering place.

Timothy followed the deer's example; getting down awkwardly on his stomach, he stuck his face in the stream and drank deeply. The water tasted vaguely leafy, or the way he imagined leaves would taste. After a lifetime of bottled or chlorinated water, it was strange and unpleasant on his tongue. Still, it was water, and he had been a long time without any.

When he had quenched his thirst he began to look around for some sheltered spot where he could spend the night. On the opposite bank he spotted a huge tree which, uprooted, had fallen across several boulders, leaving about two feet of clearance between the tree and the ground—a ready-made den. Timothy slipped off his boots and socks and, rolling up the legs of his pants, stepped into the stream. The icy water made him clench his teeth; he waded as quickly as he could across the slippery rocks.

On the far side, he stepped into his boots again and

set about improving the shelter a little. Digging out the sticks and rocks that littered the ground beneath the tree, he then turned to a nearby evergreen and, with the ax, stripped it of all the limbs within reach. Some he spread for his mattress, some he laid atop the tree and the adjacent rocks for a roof.

By the time he finished, he had neither enough strength nor enough daylight left to do anything but crawl into his shelter to sleep. Sleep was a long time coming. Evidently the pioneers knew something about the construction of pine-bough beds that he did not. The cut ends of the branches poked his ribs no matter which way he turned. When he put on his down vest, which had been serving as his pillow, it cushioned him a little, and eventually he drifted off.

Sometime in the night he awoke, chilled through, and with a wrenching pain in his gut. The first thought his groggy mind produced was: appendicitis. "Mom!" he called, sitting up and abruptly knocking his head on the tree trunk, which reminded him emphatically where he was and that neither his mother nor anyone else could hear. He lay back with his legs doubled up against his chest, groaning softly between chattering teeth. Of all the possible deaths he imagined the wilds held for him, this one hadn't even occurred to him.

What was the recommended treatment for a ruptured appendix? Obviously a shirttail bandage wasn't going to help a whole lot. So what did he do next?

The answer wasn't long in coming. What he had to do next was find a bathroom—and fast. Scrambling out of the shelter, he stumbled through the dark—unable to straighten up, yet unable to bend his bad leg—as far away as he reasonably could, which was maybe five or six yards.

Now the true nature of his malady became obvious. He thought of the leafy-tasting river water and wondered if deer were subject to diarrhea. Probably not. Nor, he imagined, did they worry much about what to use for toilet paper. After considering a moment, and rummaging through his pockets, he came up with *Lord of the Flies,* then quickly put it back. That would be sacrilege. And yet, what choice did he have? Hesitantly, he drew the book out again. After all, he had read up to about page twenty-five, so what did it really matter? Wincing, he took hold of the first few sheets and tore them carefully from the book; it was almost like pulling teeth.

By the time morning came, he had used up the entire Foreword and a dozen pages of the text, and slept a total of maybe two hours. He was too weak to drag himself out of the shelter, he was more dehydrated than ever, and, despite the constant, awful ache in his belly, he was famished. He was also more lost, if that was possible. Things were certainly going from bad to worse.

The only thing he could think of to do was read. It didn't solve anything, but it made everything more bearable, somehow, as if there were someone else here with him. If it was true that misery loves company, he was certainly miserable, and his favorite company had always been a book.

He had no idea how many hours he lay there with the book six inches from his nearsighted eyes, alternately reading and dozing, but eventually he noticed that the light seemed to be going. Reflexively, he checked his watch. Five-twenty, the same as always.

He would have poked his head out to check the sun's height, but it would have been too much effort, so he went on reading. He was coming to the point in the book now at which the boys decide to build a signal fire atop the mountain. Something clicked suddenly in Timothy's brain. A signal fire? Of course! What a dumbbell, not to have thought of it before! He was clear out of the shelter, lugging the ax, before it occurred to him that he had no means whatsoever of lighting a fire. He gave his pockets a half-hearted going-over in the faint hope that he might have absent-mindedly stuck a pack of matches in one of them at some time, the way he had stashed the book away. No such luck.

He slumped down on top of one of the boulders. Well, surely there were other ways of starting fires. Friction, for one thing. Flint and steel, for another. The Indians did it, after all, and the pioneers. But then of course they built pine-bough beds that did not resemble torture racks, and baskets that held together, too.

The book. Maybe the book would give him some idea how to go about it. Pulling it out, he read on from

---

where he had left off. Sure enough, a few pages later, there it was. Timothy knocked himself on the head. What was the matter with him? It was so simple and obvious. They used a pair of eyeglasses like a magnifying glass to focus the sun's rays on a pile of tinder.

Hastily, Timothy tucked the book away and, scrambling about, scraped up a good-sized pile of dead leaves and twigs. Smugly, he held up one of the halves of his glasses. All he had to do now was produce a tiny image of the sun and focus it on the tinder. There was just one problem—the sun wasn't cooperating. Frowning, Timothy leaned back and glared up at the heavens. No wonder the light had seemed to be fading—the sky that had been so clear and starry all night long was now blanketed with furry gray clouds, like the lint trap in his mom's dryer. "Peachy," he said, in disgust. "Just peachy."

Well, at least he'd had the good sense to make a shelter for himself. Now, if he had just had the sense not to throw away the last of his food. He glanced up at the clouds again, wondering if he had time to hobble back up to where he had dropped the basket before the rain came. Of course, as far as that went, it wouldn't hurt him to get a little wet—at least not nearly as much as starving to death would.

After cutting a stout walking stick for himself, he laid the ax inside the shelter. Slipping off the down vest, he placed it next to the ax. He forded the river in his bare feet, replaced his shoes on the far bank, and started slowly up the trail. Though the leg still felt stiff and sore, the day's rest had done it a lot of good, and he managed the steep climb fairly well, except for having to stop and rest every five minutes. Maybe he could even backtrack far enough to recover some of the berries that had leaked out.

The prospect of a meal, however limited, cheered him a little, and he found himself feeling more optimistic about his chances for survival and rescue than he had felt all day. He even began to consider what a rousing story all his tribulations would make when he got home.

Now . . . where exactly had he pitched that basket? It wasn't long after the trail had started to grow steep, so it couldn't be much farther. He scanned the brush on either side of the path as he walked.

A sudden, startling noise took his eyes from the ground around him to the hillside before him, and he stopped dead in his tracks. Not twenty yards ahead on the trail, completely blocking it, was a huge black shape, clawing at a small white one. Timothy squinted, trying to make out what it was, though his pounding heart seemed already to know: It was the bear, making shredded birch bark out of his berry basket.

SIX

GULPING, TIMOTHY STARTED SLOWLY BACKWARD. His legs were trembling so violently that he could barely have stayed on his feet even if the trail had been perfectly level; as it was, he got no more than ten steps before he slipped and his legs went out from under him. He caught himself with his hands and scrambled to his feet again, but made enough noise in the process to wake the dead. Timothy heard the bear grunt, and he caught a glimpse of the animal rearing up on its hind legs, looking as tall as the trees, before he spun around and began half-running, half-sliding down the slope.

It had started to rain now, and the leaves turned slick as waxed paper under his feet. The back of his neck prickled, waiting to feel the swipe of a great paw. He couldn't be bothered to stay on the trail this time, but crashed through brush and briers all the way to the creek, which he forded complete with socks and shoes, and at such a headlong run that he wasn't even sure his feet got wet. He didn't slow up until he reached his shelter, and even then he barely checked himself but rolled under the log, grabbed the ax, and turned to face his pursuer.

The bear was nowhere in sight. Timothy lay there, gasping for breath, soaked with rain and sweat, and peered out, expecting at any moment to see the animal come galloping across the creek, snarling, spraying water from its huge paws.

When minute after long minute went by and the animal didn't appear, Timothy started to relax a little, but far from completely; there was always the possibility that the bear was hiding out there somewhere, biding its time, waiting for him to show himself. It might even be circling around to come upon him from behind, and might at any second plunge a massive paw through his flimsy roof.

Certainly the boughs he had laid offered scant protection; even the rain had no trouble finding its way in. The main function of the evergreen thatching seemed to be to collect the thousands of little drops into hundreds of big ones, which splattered like water bombs when they hit him.

Timothy tried to scrunch himself up directly under the fallen tree itself, but that was hardly better, for the raindrops slid down the sides of the trunk and let go all in a line, wetting a single cold path down the center of his body. Finally he turned on his side and managed to escape most of the water—except for what seeped in underneath him. He did keep his down vest—and the book in its pocket—more or less dry by tucking it under the edge of one of the boulders.

Eventually it occurred to him how foolish it was to lie here cursing the rain and simultaneously dying for want of pure water. The trouble was, he had no way of collecting the rain. He knew his father should have let him buy that collapsible drinking cup.

There had to be a way to do it, something more efficient than just sticking his mouth outside. As wet as his clothes were, he could practically slake his thirst just by wringing them out over his face. As a matter of fact, that wasn't such a bad idea.

Unbuttoning his shirt, Timothy wriggled awkwardly out of it and thrust it into the rain. When it was well soaked, he drew it back inside, bunched it up, and, holding it over his mouth, twisted it tight. A good deal of the water just poured over his face, but some of it found its way into his mouth. It wasn't the best-tasting drink he'd ever had—a little on the sweaty side—but at least it wasn't likely to give him diarrhea. He repeated the maneuver a couple more times, until he was more or less satisfied, and completely drenched.

Just in case he should grow thirsty again, the rain was considerate enough to continue the rest of the day and into the night. Well, at least it might discourage the bear.

A little before dark, deciding he couldn't possibly get any wetter, Timothy crawled out of the shelter and set about cutting squares of birch bark, to make improvements on the shelter. Though the bark sheets tended to curl up at the edges, by laying rocks and dead limbs over them, he managed to create a fairly watertight roof. Then he spread a layer of bark for a floor and carefully slid in on top of it. As an afterthought, he crawled back out into the drizzle and cut a couple more squares, which he laid out over himself as a sort of blanket.

Now, if only his clothes were dry. . . . Probably he should have shingled the roof when he first saw the sky clouding up. His father, true to the Boy Scout motto, would have had it snug and seamless long before the first drop fell. His father . . .

Where was his father? Had he given up? Got lost himself? Got eaten by the bear? It had been—how long?—two full days now since he left camp. It seemed longer. It seemed like weeks since they were home in Elmira. Would his father have thought to call his mom to let her know what had happened? Probably not. He wouldn't want to upset her. It made Timothy feel funny to think of her sitting home, carrying on as usual, maybe worrying a little but not suspecting that he was really in trouble. She was probably sitting in front of the TV and simultaneously filling in a crossword puzzle with the wrong words about now. She was always trying to improve her vocabulary so she wouldn't be so embarrassed when she was out among people. As far as Timothy could see, it didn't do much good, because she clammed up in front of company anyway and let his father do all the talking—which seemed to suit his father fine.

Timothy took after his mom in that respect, he guessed. He'd almost as soon face that bear out there as he would a room full of people. Well, that was one thing that could be said for the woods. It didn't make many social demands. Yawning, Timothy curled up with his knees to his wet, cold chest and waited for morning.

When he woke, the rain had stopped, but the sky was no less gloomy. If the sun was up yet, it wasn't letting on. Shivering, Timothy climbed out from under the log and pulled the down vest on over his still-damp T-shirt. When he got to his feet, he realized suddenly that he felt absolutely terrible; his head and his joints ached, his throat was raw, his sinuses throbbed. His first impulse was to slink back into the shelter and stay there. But common sense told him that if he didn't dry out and get something in his stomach, he would only get weaker and more sick.

The only way he knew of to get dry in the absence of sun or fire was to start walking, which he would have to do anyway if he wanted to find food. Oddly enough, he felt almost reluctant to leave the shelter. It wasn't much, but it was home of a sort, and there was no way of telling what lay downriver. Still, if he stayed he had the bear to worry about. And he couldn't sit in one spot forever anyway. What if no one ever came for him? Maybe they'd figure it wasn't even worth it, sending out choppers and planes and men after one insignificant kid. After all, nobody had ever thought him worth bothering with before—why would they start now?

Maybe it was better just to assume that his fate was in his own blistered hands.

Sighing and sneezing, he shouldered the ax, to which he had tied his wet shirt, and started along the creek in the same direction the water flowed. His wet pants chafed his legs so that he was forced to walk bowlegged. But at least the injured leg was in better shape now; he could flex it a little without feeling that it was going to split the wound wide open.

Since this bank of the river was mostly flat, the going was not particularly rough, except for an occasional detour around a clump of bushes that overhung the water and a few small rivulets that crossed his path to empty into the larger creek. Most of these were narrow enough to step across, and the one that wasn't boasted a natural footbridge in the form of a fallen tree.

From time to time he heard some sound beside or behind him, or maybe across the river, and he tensed and walked more gingerly, listening for a growl or the tread of heavy paws. Then, after a minute, he relaxed again and walked on in his usual noisy manner, crunching twigs and sneezing loudly.

The morning flowed by as smoothly as the river, without incident—unless the sun finally deciding to show itself could be called an incident. Otherwise all that happened was that he walked and rested, walked and rested.

By the time the sun peaked in the sky, his clothes were dry again; so, unfortunately, was his throat. Before long, it had grown so warm that he had to remove the vest. He had hoped to come across more berries, but evidently they didn't flourish on the river banks. He passed a few unfamiliar bushes laden with small, shiny red fruit that seemed to attract a number of sparrows, but one wary taste was enough to tell him that the berries were strictly for the birds.

The only other thing he came across that resembled food was a number of sardine-sized minnows darting about in a still pool separated from the rain-swollen river by a sandbar. If there were small fish, it stood to reason there must be bigger ones, too. He might even be able to rig up some sort of fishing tackle, but the problem still remained of how to cook his catch. He had read somewhere that Oriental people ate raw fish —but then they ate thousand-year-old eggs, too.

Then, late in the day, as he stretched his tired legs across a small tributary, he caught a glimpse of something that made him pause—a large mass of bright green choked the mouth of the inlet. Kneeling on the damp ground, Timothy plucked a sprig of the vegetation. Though he was certainly no botanist, he had never heard of any sort of plant that would grow right out of a stream that way, except watercress. Hesitantly, he nipped off a leaf and chewed it. It had a strong but not unpleasant peppery taste. As he stuck his hand in to pull up another bunch, he noticed how frigid the water felt. Could that mean it was spring water? Taking a mouthful of the watercress, he stood and pushed his way though the weeds and bushes.

Only a few yards off, he found the source of the tiny

stream. It welled steadily from a cave-like depression where the ground started to slope upward. "Well, what do you know," Timothy said aloud. Crouching, he cupped a handful of the icy water and, remembering the results of his last drink of river water, sipped at it tentatively, apprehensively. It was so cold that it had no taste at all; it seemed to numb his entire mouth. He drank again and again. Well, between the possibly pure water and the possible watercress, either he was going to be well-fed and watered, or else he was going to be subject to severe dysentery and terminal food poisoning.

When he had drunk so much that his gullet felt frozen, he moved back down to the river and, lying down in the grass, finished filling his stomach with watercress.

Overhead the rain clouds seemed to be regrouping for another attack. Unless he wanted to spend another miserable night, it was time to start working on a shelter. Since there were no birch trees of any size here, he began cutting evergreen boughs. When he had more than he thought he could ever possibly need, he lopped off a long sapling, leaned it against a tree, and placed layer upon layer of branches against it on both sides, to form a sort of A-frame structure. By the time he used up all he had cut, it was nearly dark. Hastily, he rounded up enough moss from the hillside to cushion the ground a little, and then, regretfully patting the book that still lay unread in his vest pocket, he crawled inside the cramped shelter.

He stretched out with a groan of exhaustion and was on the verge of dropping off to sleep when it occurred to him that he had not dug the obligatory runoff ditch. Torn between taking his dose of misery now, in the form of more work, or later, in the form of a soaked bed, he sighed and, crawling back outside, scraped a shallow trench along the two uphill sides of his evergreen tent with the butt of the ax. At a depth of about one inch, he mumbled, "Good enough," and gave up.

This time he was asleep almost before he got all the way inside the shelter. For a change, even the cold—either the one in his head or the drop in temperature—failed to wake him through the night.

SEVEN

TOWARD DAWN, Timothy woke and for a moment was sure, seeing the triangular shape above him, that he was back in the nylon tent. Had his father found him at last and carried him back, unconscious, to the camp? He reached out and touched the dark roof; it prickled his skin and brought him back to reality.

Timothy raised himself up on one elbow, trying to place the sound he kept hearing. The river, of course. He lay back, nodding. It was a comforting sort of sound, like that of voices talking softly in the next room after you've gone to bed.

But there was something else, a sound like pages being riffled in a book or . . . or rain falling on evergreen boughs. That was it—it was raining on his shelter, and he wasn't even getting wet.

"All right!" he said under his breath, grinning. It looked like at long last he'd managed to do something more or less right. It was good that he qualified the thought with a "more or less," for just then a large drop landed in the middle of his grin. Oh, well—what was one drop, or twenty, even? The important thing was, he was more dry than wet.

He lay there for what must have been an hour or more, just listening to the faint flutter of the rain on his pine-needle thatching. It was even more pleasant than the murmur of the river. He was almost disappointed when it stopped. Still, it was just as well. The moss bed was beginning to feel unbearably hard and lumpy—he'd have to work on that. Besides, the sun was up; it was time to move on if he ever wanted to find his way out of here. He smiled at his own eagerness to be up. Back home, he had never been in bed before eleven and never out of it before seven-thirty. On weekends bedtime was usually after *The Late Show,* and morning came about ten or eleven. Lately, he was probably even beating his father—wherever he was—out of bed.

Slowly, scratching his head and yawning, Timothy emerged from the shelter. The woods were dark and drenched. A mist rose from the surface of the river, as if it were steaming hot. He wished it were, and that he had a tea bag, and a couple of eggs to soft-boil. He could have stood to steep himself in hot water a couple of hours, too.

Things being what they were, the best he could do was a few handfuls of spring water to drink, a few more to wash—and numb—his face, and a side order of watercress. Now that he was fairly certain the water was potable and the cress edible, it would make sense to haul as much of both with him as he could. He felt sure he could make a serviceable basket this time, but a water bucket—that was a toughie.

He cut two squares of bark from the largest birch he could find. From one square he fashioned a basket similar to the berry basket, but held together at the corners with twigs split up the middle and clamped on clothespin-style.

After staring at the second square for a few minutes, he tried rolling it up in a cylinder about three inches across. Then he pinched the bottom closed and stuck another split stick crossways on it, tying up the split end of the "clothespin" with tough grass stems. It looked good. But when he dipped it in the spring and held it up, the water fairly streamed from it. He obviously needed some kind of sealer. What did the old reliable Indians use? Hiawatha, for instance? He'd used something to stop up the seams of his canoe. Spruce gum?

Timothy wandered around for a half-hour looking for something resembling spruce gum, or his idea of it. Finally he found a couple of teaspoonfuls of sticky resin oozing out of an evergreen that looked like just a pine to him. Scraping it off, he poked it into the seam at the bottom of the bucket. A couple more globs of it, and he had the crack pretty well caulked—not to mention his fingers. When he returned to the spring and dipped in the bucket a second time, the bottom didn't leak— the sides did. Back to the tree, and another bit of caulking, then back to the spring. This time the leakage was reduced to an occasional drip. Now, if it just had a handle. That would take some thought. For now, he filled the bucket with water and the basket with watercress and tucked one under each arm. With a last satisfied glance at the snug shelter, he started off downstream.

The leg hardly bothered him at all, now. The first time he stopped to rest, he unwrapped the bandage and stuffed it in his vest pocket. Except for a little soreness and a puffy redness along it, the gash seemed to be mending nicely. He wished he could do as much for the rip in his jeans. He was forever snagging it on something.

His cold, too, was on the mend. His main complaint now was a constant headache, probably due to hunger, and a stiff neck from the sleeping accommodations. Still, overall, he felt better than he would have expected. Certainly he was a long way from dead, which is what everyone would have most likely given him up for by now. Maybe when he got home he wouldn't even show himself at first, but just sneak around and listen in on what people were saying about him, the way Tom Sawyer and Huck did.

If only he could somehow let just his mother know he was okay. He didn't like to think of her worrying over him all this time. Maybe it wouldn't be much longer. Say he made five or six miles a day, and it was twenty or thirty to civilization, like his father had said. That meant a maximum of maybe . . . six days, and he'd already put in a day and a half. Of course the direction he was going, it might be more like fifty miles, or sixty, to a town or even an isolated house. The thing was, he was bound to hit one sooner or later, and as long as he could find pure water to drink and a little food, he was pretty sure now that he could make it.

Timothy became aware, as the day went on, that the stream he was following was growing deeper and slower-moving, and its bed turning less rocky and more sandy. Occasionally he stopped and sat on the bank for a few minutes, to see if he could spot any fish swimming in the clear water. He never saw anything that looked longer than his finger.

But during a rest stop sometime in the middle of the afternoon, he noticed something else. At first he took them to be scattered rocks lying on the bottom, but upon closer examination, they looked too uniformly oval. Curious, he set his bark containers aside, slipped off his shoes and socks, and waded into the chilly stream, wincing as he set his foot down on a sharp rock.

Bending down, he picked up one of the dark, flat shapes. It moved slightly in his hand, closing up a crack along its side. Timothy jumped and almost dropped it. "Clams!" he said aloud. "How about that!"

Sloshing back to the bank, he sat down to look over his find. Here was a possible meal, if he could manage to get it open. Dredging up his knife-fork-spoon, he unfolded the blade and, working the point between the halves of the shell, he twisted. Much as Timothy himself used to do at the doctor's office, the clam refused to open its mouth, giving a new vividness to the phrase "to clam up." Well, he could be stubborn, too. "Say ahh," Timothy grunted, and pried harder. At last the clam yielded and the shell gave way. "Hmm." Inside, it certainly didn't look edible, not at all the way clams in a container of clam dip looked. Unfolding his spoon, Timothy gingerly scooped out the contents of the shell. His stomach was seized alternately by nausea and pangs of hunger. If he just had a small fire, he could chop the little devil up—into what? Well, a small fire and a cookpot, then. Might as well wish for a few potatoes and some cream and a little parsley while he was at it.

The fact was, it was either eat it raw or forget it. Cleaning off some of the more suspect parts, he squeezed his eyes shut, opened his mouth, popped the clam in, and swallowed. Despite its general sliminess, it seemed to stick in his throat. Eventually, though, he got it down and it promised to stay there.

As with so many things, after the first time it got easier. When he had consumed a dozen or so and they lay like so many stones in his stomach, he waded around gathering a couple more handfuls, which he tucked in his basket among the bunches of watercress. It looked almost attractive, rather like a grocer's display.

As he sat brushing the sand from his feet, he noticed a cut on the sole of his left foot, the result, no doubt, of his painful encounter with the sharp rock. Though it stung a little, it was nothing major; he pulled on his footgear and started off, planning to put a few more miles behind him before stopping for the night.

Plans, like rules and promises, are made to be broken. He walked for no more than ten minutes before he was faced with an obstacle. Up until now, he had been very lucky as far as the terrain was concerned. A few times he had been forced to circle around some particularly dense patch of brush or scramble across a sandbar or a cutaway bank, but for the most part the ground had been fairly firm and level, and the undergrowth manageable. Now, suddenly, the valley was narrowing and the bank he was on was becoming as high and steep as the opposite bank. There was nothing to do but climb to higher ground. The thought made his stomach knot up. As long as he had stayed in sight of the river, he couldn't get lost—or at least more lost. What happened if he made a wide detour and then couldn't find his way back to the stream? It seemed unlikely, but then it had seemed unlikely that he would get lost just going out to cut firewood, too.

Cut firewood! His stomach took another jolt of panic. The ax! Where was the ax? He had used it that morning, to cut the bark for the containers, and then . . . and then he had left it leaning against the birch tree, back by the spring.

EIGHT

TIMOTHY SANK DOWN in the grass, suddenly overcome by weakness. How could he have done such a stupid thing? Because it was the kind of thing he always did, that was why. Here he was, thinking he was in command of the situation because he'd built some dinky shelter.

Well, that was the last one he'd build. He couldn't very well put up a shelter without an ax. He sat there, nervously and aimlessly yanking clumps of grass out of the ground, trying to decide whether to go back or go on. If he returned, it meant better than a full day lost, even if he hustled. If he went on, he'd be at the mercy of the elements. Sighing, he looked up the river, then down it. "Eenie, meenie, minie, mo," he said, pointing one way, then the other. "My, mother, told, me, to, pick, this, one." Downstream. Okay. Well, his mother had never lied to him before. Picking up his food and water, he got to his feet. Maybe there was a village just over the hill. North Wilmurt, maybe.

He gave a last glance upstream, then started climbing the slope, away from the river. Though the bank wasn't quite as steep here as it was farther along, it was no picnic, either. Several times he slipped in the loose dirt, or rocks gave way under his feet, making him stumble and spill water from his birch bucket. By the time he reached the crest of the ridge, his bad leg had begun to ache again, and half his water supply was gone —or, at any rate, had been transferred to his pants and shirt.

But at least the going was easier now. Stands of huge trees, in the shade of which nothing grew but moss and ferns, alternated with sunny natural glades where dozens of varieties of grasses and tiny flowers flourished. There were several kinds of mushrooms, too, and he was tempted to nibble at the more appetizing-looking ones, but he had read too many dire warnings about poisonous fungi to risk it.

He steered to his left as much as possible, back toward the river, but always something blocked his way —a crevice in the ground, an impassable copse of young evergreens—and for a long while he lost sight of the water completely. When he finally completed his semicircle and emerged on a hilltop overlooking the river again, a whole new vista met his eyes. The valley widened abruptly here, and the stream was no longer a stream—it paused in the broad plain to become a lake, or a bog, more accurately, for grass-covered hillocks and isolated clumps of trees projected here and there over much of its surface. At the far end, Timothy saw what looked like a beaver dam—which would explain the number of pointed stumps dotting the area—and beyond that the stream continued, winding lazily along until it disappeared in the distant trees. No sign of a road, or power line, or a habitation—unless you counted the beaver lodge.

Well, he hadn't really expected anything, anyway, not this soon. Besides, a road or a house would have looked somehow . . . out of place here. It was so unspoiled and so—he had to admit it—so beautiful, sort of like a really great paint-by-number—not the kind his mom did—made of swatches of grassy green and watery silver-blue and the reflected orange of the sinking sun. He stood there on the hilltop, just looking down on the scene for several minutes. Then, realizing how near it was to dusk, he hurried down the slope.

The lake must have been larger at one time, for the woods did not crowd right to the edge of the water, but stood back a dozen yards or so, aloof, on higher ground. Between the water and the trees lay a sort of meadow of lush grass, half green with this year's growth, half yellow with that of previous years. Timothy walked around aimlessly at the edge of the woods, trying to think what to do about shelter, before it occurred to him that the answer might be right at his feet. He stepped into the trees, making plans in his head as he went. There was no shortage of dead wood, and he picked out two fallen saplings, broke off the brittle small branches, and dragged the trunks out into the meadow.

There he broke one sapling into two lengths of about four or five feet each, which he stuck into the soft earth with the bottoms several feet apart and the tops together, in an A-shape. The second sapling he snapped off at a length of ten or twelve feet and, placing one end on the ground, he set the other end in the notch at the peak of the A. Now what he needed was something to tie the three ends together. He scratched his head, glanced around for a while, and finally spotted some vines climbing up, and nearly choking, a nearby tree. With some effort he pulled one of the long, clinging tendrils down and proceeded to wrap it around and around the three pieces of his shelter frame where they crossed, until they were bound firmly together. Now for the sides. Moving down to the edge of the lake, he gathered several armfuls of dead, woody stems which were all that remained of some tall weed whose season was past. He laid the sticklike stems up against his ridgepole to form a sort of tent. Well, so far so good.

He next set about gathering armload after armload of the dead yellow grass. Some he spread inside the shelter, the rest he laid in horizontal bundles atop the vertical woody stems to make a thatched roof. Now, how was he going to keep the thatch in place? The easiest answer, at least for now, seemed to be just to lay dead limbs atop the grass. He could always perfect the design later.

When he finished, it was almost too dark to see his handiwork; but perhaps it was just as well. It appeared to be a rather unlovely structure. Still, he had done it himself, unaided by tools or instructions, and inside it was snug, almost pleasant. The roof and floor smelled musty and yet faintly sweet. The open end of the shelter looked out over the lake, which seemed somehow to hold the last light of day, making it appear almost luminescent.

For a long time, Timothy sat gazing at the water, which was stirred occasionally by some fish or beaver tail, and ate watercress and a few of the clams. They improved with the growing darkness, since he could devour them without having to look at them.

Though he was worn out from the long day's hike and the hurried shelter-building, he didn't feel like simply collapsing, as he had on previous nights. After a while the moon rose, and he sat watching its reflection on the lake and listening to the cry of some lonesome bird and to the crickets' song. Finally, too weary to keep his eyes open, he lay back on the soft, dry grass.

NINE

THE FIRST THING he was aware of in the morning was pain. There were the usual aches in joints and muscles, of course, but there was also a hunger that chewed fiercely at his belly, not to mention a throbbing pain in his left foot. He sat up, grimacing, squinting into the early sun, and took a gulp of spring water to temporarily thwart the hunger pangs. A gulp was all that remained —the rest had apparently seeped out of the container during the night. Timothy glanced at the food basket. Neither the watercress, which was wilted and slimy, nor the clams, which were gaping open slightly, looked at all appetizing.

Scooting forward to the front of the shelter, he pulled off his sock to have a look at his aching foot. The small, innocuous cut he had noticed the day before was now red and swollen and excruciatingly tender to the touch. "Oh, wonderful," he groaned. A fat lot of miles he was going to make walking on that. Sighing, he sat looking across the lake. Maybe he ought to just stay put for a while. This was about the clearest area he'd come across, the one where he'd be most likely to be spotted from the air—provided anybody was still looking for him. Surely they were still looking. Surely. But if they were . . . *where were they?*

For the first time in several days, he felt the panic return, grabbing hold of his stomach more savagely than the hunger, worse than the dysentery. It swept over him like an icy wind and, doubling up on the floor of the shelter, he began to cry uncontrollably.

When he could cry no more, he lay exhausted, both relieved—all the built-up fears and miseries of the past days were behind the outburst—and ashamed. His father would have called him a baby, if he'd seen it. But it wasn't true; he wasn't a baby. He'd done all right up to now. After all, he was still alive . . . no thanks to his father. Why hadn't he come yet? Where was he?

Timothy shook his head. No. He wasn't going to start thinking like that again. He needed to keep his mind clear, to solve the problems he still faced: how to get food, and water, and how to signal any aircraft that might pass overhead.

Hearing a slight rustle in the grass outside the shelter, Timothy lifted his head a little to look, keeping the rest of his body still. Not ten feet away sat a rabbit, gazing curiously at him, twitching its nose. At first, he smiled, amazed at how close it had approached. Chances were it had never seen a human being before.

Then his smile faded as it dawned on him that this

was not just a cute visitor from the animal world—it was food. Trying not to make any sudden moves, he groped surreptitiously about under the matted grass with one hand, trying to locate one of the rocks that had seemed so plentiful, and so huge, under his spine the night before. Finally he touched cold stone; digging at it with his fingertips, he dislodged it and drew it slowly to him.

Springing up suddenly, he flung the missile. In the same instant, the rabbit came to life and turned to flee. Incredibly, the stone caught it in the ribs, bowling it over. The rabbit scrabbled around wildly, trying to regain its feet, but before it managed Timothy was upon it, grabbing its hind legs. It jerked and squealed and doubled up, trying to bite his hand, startling him so that he very nearly dropped it.

Timothy looked around him frantically. What in heaven's name did he do now? Slit its throat? Wring its neck? Bewildered, he abruptly slung its head against the ground, wanting to make it stop its pitiful struggling and pleading. The rabbit went limp and silent.

For a moment, Timothy held the slack form in his hands, as stunned as if he had been the one whose head was knocked on the ground. When he saw that the animal was indeed dead, he crouched and laid it gently on the grass. So this was how the hunter felt. If it was, why did anyone ever hunt?

He tried to tell himself that he was wrong to feel so sorrowful, so sorry. This was the way of things: some animals died so that others could live. After all, he had eaten hamburgers and hot dogs almost all his life, and they weren't made out of sawdust. Still, it wasn't the same—not at all like having to look the animal in the eye and kill it with your own hands.

Timothy sniffed and laid a hand on the rabbit's soft fur. His father would really say he was being a baby now, making such a big deal about killing an animal, especially considering how much he needed the food.

Well, if it was dead anyway, he probably ought to make use of it. If he didn't that meant it would have died for no reason, and that would be even worse.

There were two rather major problems here, though. One was that he had no idea how to go about skinning the rabbit—the carcass; it was easier if he thought of it that way. The second hitch was that he still had no fire to cook it with. Fingering the knife-fork-spoon in his pocket, he glanced at the carcass. Maybe it would be a good idea to start the fire first and let the skinning go until later. Yes. Now that he thought about it, that would definitely be best.

With a sense of relief, he backed away from the dead rabbit and sat down in the opening of the shelter. The one sock he had on was soaked with dew. Gritting his teeth, he pulled the other sock on carefully over his infected foot. Getting the shoe on was a little more tricky, and there was no way of walking without some pain. He hobbled into the woods, trying to favor the cut knee and the infected foot simultaneously, and succeeding only in aggravating them both.

He made several limping trips between the shelter

and the woods, first rounding up a supply of dry birch bark and small twigs for tinder, then dragging out some bigger branches meant to keep the blaze going, provided he should ever get one started. Finally, deciding he had enough fuel, he set about pulling up handfuls of grass to make a cleared area for the fire.

It wasn't until he sat down for a brief rest that it occurred to him he hadn't seen the rabbit lately. He glanced around, puzzled. Now what had he done with it? He could have sworn he had left it lying in the grass in front of the shelter, but maybe he had put it inside. He checked. Nothing but smelly clams and dried-up watercress and an empty water bucket. Licking his dry lips, he backed out and searched the area around the shelter.

There was no question—for whatever reason, by whatever means, the rabbit was gone. Had some other animal—a fox, maybe—dragged it off in his absence? Or maybe . . . maybe it had just been playing possum and, as soon as he was out of sight, had sprung up and bounded away, alive and well. After all, he hadn't really hit it all that hard. Though his stomach put in a dissenting vote, overall he couldn't help feeling glad that the rabbit was gone. He wasn't at all sure he could have brought himself to skin it.

Of course, that still left the problem of what he was going to eat. Fish seemed a good possibility—he was sure he'd seen some jumping last evening. Well, if he could manage to catch one, he was still going to need a fire; he turned back to that task.

When he had a circle of bare ground about four feet across, he made a pile of twigs and shredded bark, and drew out one half of his eyeglasses. This time the sun was high and hot, and he fiddled with the lens until he produced a tiny likeness of the sun on a piece of the tinder. Grinning in anticipation, he waited for the dry bark to burst into flame. It refused to so much as smoke. Frowning a little, he adjusted the position of the lens. He waited. Nothing. Come on. What was he doing wrong? He shifted his cramped legs, wiped the sweat from his forehead, sat down, and focused the spot of sun again, with no more success.

Was he using the wrong kind of tinder? He tried dry grass; he split up the end of a stick into toothpicks with his knife; he focused on brown pine needles and brown leaves, all with the same results—which was to say, no results at all.

Was the lens at fault, maybe? The kid in the book had had really bad eyesight; presumably his lenses would have been thicker. Or maybe the author had just made the whole thing up, without bothering to check it out. That wasn't playing fair. Of course, a Western writer couldn't reasonably be expected to shoot himself just to see how it felt, or a science fiction writer to wait until he could book passage on a spaceship in order to write about interstellar travel. But it seemed like if you wanted to do a realistic book, you owed it to the reader to make sure the stuff your hero did could actually be done.

Disgusted, he stuck the glasses in his pocket. Now

what? Rub two sticks together? Or was that just another made-up method? Flint and steel? He knew more or less what flint looked like from seeing arrowheads at the college science museum. Whether he could recognize it in its natural state was another question.

The answer, as it turned out, was no. He limped around for an hour or so, picking up a few likely-looking stones near the lake but, when struck against his closed knife blade, none of them made a self-respecing spark. Discouraged, he flung them, one by one, into the lake.

The last one raised an answering splash, like an echo. A fish—it had to be. So, they were sitting out there, waiting to be caught. If they jumped at a stone, they ought to do flip-flops for a worm. All he had to do was figure out a way to cook them.

Timothy vigorously scratched his head, which was light and unsteady from hunger. Think. A magnifying glass would burn a hole in wood; he knew that from having done it a summer camp. He also knew a magnifying lens was a double-convex, that is, rounded on both sides. Pulling out his glasses, he examined the lenses. They were convex on the outside, concave on the inside. Tentatively, he pressed the two inside surfaces together and held them up to catch the sun. He focused the tiny ball of light on his hand. A second later, he jerked the hand away. "Ow!" Well, at least he was on the right track. If he could somehow glue the lenses in place like that, and maybe fill the space between them with water to make a solid lens . . . it probably still wouldn't work. On the other hand, maybe it was worth a try. He sure had nothing better to do, and the glasses weren't much account the way they were, anyway.

He took out his knife-fork-spoon and, holding the glasses close to his face so he could see what he was doing, he painstakingly unscrewed the hinge screws from both sides. Sticking the lenses in his pocket, he limped off to look for more spruce gum, or pine pitch, or whatever he had used to caulk the water bucket.

It took him a good hour or more. As he headed back through the woods toward the shelter with a couple of ounces of resin on a birch-bark platter, he noticed, as he passed under a large deciduous tree, a number of round, hard objects pressing into the sole of his left foot painfully at every step.

Halting, he bent down and, raking away the fallen, windblown leaves of past summers, uncovered a trove of small nuts, some enclosed in fat burrs, some bare and roughly pyramid-shaped. He rounded up two flat stones and, kneeling, smashed a nut between them. The insides were black and shriveled. "Phooey!" Reaching up, he plucked a nut from the tree itself, knocked the hull loose, cracked it. This one held a small, whitish kernel which he dug out with his knife and hesitantly tasted. It wasn't great—a little on the bitter side—but it wasn't bad, either. Grabbing a low branch, he shook it vigorously; a hail of nuts descended on him.

Laughing, he cracked them and popped them into his mouth as fast as he could—and came near to chucking them up again. He forced himself to sit and consume them more slowly, chew them more thoroughly, and stop when he had barely made a dent in his hunger. Then, taking off his shirt, he knotted the sleeves and hobbled about, filling this makeshift bag. When he had all he could carry, he looked around, with rare foresight, for landmarks that would allow him to locate the tree again. He took note of a tall, dead pine, an odd depression in the ground, a stump that looked like a chair. Satisfied, he hefted the nuts and the bark platter of resin and headed for the shelter.

As he emerged, whistling, from the woods just above his grass hut, the sight that met his eyes made him halt, amazed, and then slip back behind a tree. He could have sworn the shelter was moving!

TEN

TIMOTHY HELD HIS DIZZY HEAD. Was he so hungry he was beginning to have hallucinations? Cautiously, he peered out from behind the tree. There was no doubt about it—the shelter was shaking and jumping as though it were atop an active earthquake fault. But it was no earthquake. Something round and black and furry projected from the entrance of the hut. "Oh, God," Timothy murmured. It was the bear again. It had followed him.

As he watched, the bear backed out of the shelter, leaving it crazily skewed and on the verge of falling down. In its jaws it held the birch basket. The animal actually looked rather comical, almost clownish, with its hindquarters stuck in the air and its forelegs splayed out on the ground. It batted the basket about for a minute, like a cat playing with a mouse, then proceeded to rip it apart and go after the clams, which by now were bound to be a little on the fragrant side—most likely what had attracted the animal in the first place.

At first, Timothy almost laughed at the bear's antics, as it tried to pry open the clams. With its intent expression, the bear looked like an oversized muscleman trying to open a delicate locket. It even stuck its tongue out at one point, like a child bent on some intricate task.

Then Timothy pictured himself in the place of the clam, and dropped back behind the tree. Was he upwind or downwind? He wet his finger and held it up; there seemed to be no wind at all. He glanced quickly at the branches overhead, looking for one that was within his reach. But hadn't he read somewhere that black bears were excellent climbers?

What he really needed was a weapon. Why, oh why, had he left the ax behind? As quietly as he could, he limped back into the woods. When he came across a suitable sapling, he set about hacking at it with the blade of his knife-fork-spoon, jerking his head up at every sound. By the time he frayed the base of the small tree in two, he was sweating profusely and the knife blade was becoming wobbly. It took him an equally long time to trim the branches off and sharpen something of a point at the smaller end of the stick. Hefting this makeshift spear, he chucked it experimentally at a clump of moss. It flopped to the ground five feet short of the target, sending up a shower of dirt from the point. Timothy sat down wearily. Oh, well, he didn't plan on having to throw it, anyway.

So, what did he plan on doing? Go back for a duel

to the death? Hardly. Move on and try to keep ahead of the bear? Not a bad idea, except for the fact that he could scarcely walk.

What then? Stay here and build a shelter in some other location? Not much point in that. If the bear had trailed him this far, it wouldn't have any trouble seeking him out wherever he was. Why it should want to, he had no idea, but the fact was it kept turning up. Maybe it didn't like intruders in its territory. Or—the thought hadn't occurred to him before—maybe it was just curious.

Still, he couldn't take any chances. Even if they weren't downright hostile, bears were known to be dangerous; he'd read stories about them mauling tourists in Yellowstone.

One good way—at least, according to *The Jungle Book*—of keeping bears and other wild animals at a distance was to build a fire. Of course that would solve a lot of his problems. Unfortunately it was much easier said, and written about, than done. In *The Jungle Book*, the boy had just taken coals from a fire in the village. Well, heck, if there had been a village around, Timothy wouldn't *need* a fire.

There was still the double-lens idea to be tried, though he honestly didn't hold much hope for it. Still, he might just as well glue the two halves together while he was sitting here. With any luck, maybe the bear would be gone when he returned to the shelter.

It wasn't all that hard to do, since the pitch or gum was about as sticky as a person could wish. His main problem was seeing what he was doing unaided by the glasses. Finally, when he was pretty sure he had the edges well sealed except for a gap at the top, he rose and, taking up his spear and his shirtful of nuts, made his way to the edge of the woods again.

To his relief, there was no sign of the bear, except for those signs it had left behind—the shredded basket and several clam shells which, apparently having failed to pry open, the bear had simply crushed.

Warily, still carrying the spear in front of him, Timothy limped down to the water's edge and dipped in the lenses. Surprisingly, they held water. Back at the shelter, he caulked the remaining gap, dried off the outside with his undershirt, and crouched down over the pile of tinder. The sun was lower in the sky now, but still hot enough to make him sweat. He focused its image on the dry bark. Almost at once a tiny wisp of smoke went up.

Timothy blinked and brushed the perspiration from his eyes. Had he really seen smoke? He fiddled with the lens. Nothing. What was going on? He tried moving the sun spot around, and finally, when it lit on a patch of dark pine bark, he raised a fluff of smoke again. Well, that made sense: Light stuff reflected light; dark stuff absorbed it.

But where there was smoke, there was supposed to be fire. So where was the fire? Timothy bent closer and blew on the smoldering patch of tinder. No flames. Maybe he needed something more flammable—like gasoline. Or paper, even . . . But where—

He dragged his vest from the cockeyed shelter and took out *Lord of the Flies*. First toilet paper, now tinder. Shaking his head remorsefully, he tore out a half-dozen pages, crumpled them, and tucked them under the edge of the pile of bark. When he trained his lens on the black type, the paper smoked furiously and, as he blew very gently on it, it glowed and finally it burst into flame.

Timothy dropped the lens and fed the tiny flame with leaves and bits of bark. "Please don't go out," he murmured over and over, like an incantation. "Please don't go out." A bit of old Cub Scout lore flashed through his mind: build a teepee. He broke up sticks and laid them in a cone shape over the blossoming fire, small ones at first, then bigger ones—too big. The fire paused, smoldered for a heart-stopping second, and then, as Timothy yanked off the larger stuff, caught its breath and, rekindling, climbed up to devour the stick teepee.

When the fire became such an undeniable reality that it nearly singed his eyebrows, Timothy sat back, dazed and elated—and saw the bear. It stood at the edge of the lake, swaying on its hind legs, its head bobbing as it sniffed the air. Timothy got to his knees and watched it anxiously, dreamlike, through the shimmering heat waves of the fire.

On an impulse, riding on a surge of confidence, he suddenly flapped his arms and called out, shrilly, "Hah!" I am Man, Maker of Fire. "Hah!" At his first yell, the bear stared in his direction; at the second, the animal whirled abruptly, still on its hind legs, and then, dropping to all fours, loped off rather gracefully and at an almost leisurely pace. It paused once to cast a curious, unhurried glance at Timothy over its shoulder before disappearing over a rise in the ground up the valley.

Though he still had nothing to cook over the fire, it was more than welcome as a source of heat and of security through the chilly night. After a supper of nutmeats, swallowed waterless, he hobbled about until dark, gathering moss for his bed. Thanks to this and the fire's warmth, he slept soundly, almost comfortably, despite his thirst, waking only in the early hours to drag a huge dead branch onto the glowing coals. He soon wished he had stayed in bed.

As he shuffled backward, pulling at the awkward limb, he heard a sickening crunch underfoot. He knew at once what it was. "Aw, no," he wailed. He bent and picked up the shattered lenses from where he had carelessly tossed them in his first flush of triumph. Shaking his head miserably, he turned them over in his hand. Chalk up another one for Wrong-Way Tim.

Well, so much for Man, the Maker of Fire. From now on he'd have to be like prehistoric man; he'd have to make absolutely certain the fire never went out.

The rest of his night's sleep was fitful at best. In his anxiety, he built up such a blaze that the shelter became a large reflector oven, parching him, sweating out water that he had no way of replacing. When he did sleep, he dreamed that the shelter was on fire or, alternately, that he had overslept and let the fire die out. On the other hand, for a change he did not dream of bears.

ELEVEN

WHEN MORNING CAME, before he even ate, he set about gathering firewood. It was a miserable task, for he was growing weak from hunger and thirst; there was a faint buzzing in his ears. He had even more trouble walking today, too, for, although the cut knee was healing fast, the infection in his foot had spread. Small, tender red lines extended like spiders' legs from a puffy, painful center.

He made only two trips in and out of the woods, dragging enormous dead branches, before he sank, exhausted and sweating, into the grass. This was no good. As important as the fire was, if he didn't have food and water soon, he'd be nothing but well-warmed vulture bait.

Shading his eyes, he squinted up at the sky, looking not for vultures but for rain clouds. He wasn't entirely sure whether he wanted to see any or not. A good rain would mean fresh drinking water, but it would probably also mean the end of his fire. Well, his feelings on the matter were neither here nor there anyway, since there wasn't a cloud in sight.

Sighing, he pulled the bag of nuts to him and cracked a few as he gazed out over the lake. Water, water everywhere, and not a drop to drink. He chewed reflectively on the nutmeats; they stuck in his dry throat, and he coughed until tears came to his eyes. Well, at least that proved he wasn't totally dehydrated. Just dry—so dry that he was almost willing to risk another bout with diarrhea. But there must be another way. How did a person go about purifying water? Distill it? Surely just boiling it would suffice. If he only had a container of some sort. . . . He stared thoughtfully at the mangled watercress basket. Last year, his General Science teacher had done a stunt that involved boiling water in a paper box; conceivably the same thing might work with a birch-bark box, mightn't it?

He made one more trip for wood and, in the process, brought back the birch square and the resin from the day before. It took him only a matter of minutes to whip up a decent box and caulk it—his own adeptness surprised him. A quick hobble down to the lake for water, and the dubious experiment was ready to proceed.

He made a bed of hot coals between two sizable wood chunks, set the container of water over them, and waited for it to curl up and burst into flame. It sat quietly except for the occasional drip that sizzled into the fire.

Nervously, Timothy chewed up a few more nuts while he waited. He heaped a fresh pile of coals under the box. He stuck his finger in the water and shrugged —it was lukewarm, anyway. Remembering the saying about a watched pot never boiling, he busied himself scraping bare a spot in the midst of the fire, where he tossed a handful of unhulled nuts, then covered them with hot coals.

The worst that could happen, after all, was that the box would burn—and, of course, spill the water, putting out his fire. He went back to watching again. To his astonishment, after only an eternity the water began to boil. He shoved more coals under it and kept it rolling for what he calculated was about ten minutes, according to the Song Method (one time through "The Cat Said Fiddle-i-dee" = two minutes) and then lifted it gingerly off the fire, using his vest as a potholder.

By the time the water cooled, which took another eternity, he had only kicked ashes into it twice. He poured it back and forth between the box and the bucket to cool it further, spilling perhaps a third of it, and finally, hesitantly, he quaffed a little. It was still warm, and so bitter he almost spit it back out. And yet, it was wet, and he swallowed it gratefully, though with a little difficulty.

His experiment with roasted nuts fared about the same. Half of them were charred; the other half, though tasty, were no more than an appetizer. After a short rest and a few more gulps of water, he dredged up enough energy to start wondering how to go about catching himself some fish. A pole was, of course, no problem. But fishing line and a hook . . .

The only thing he could think of that would be strong enough to land a fish was his shoelaces. With a shrug, he slipped them out of the eyelets of his hiking boots. Tied together, they made a line about ten feet long.

The hook took a little more pondering. He tried to carve one, with no success—the point kept breaking off. Finally, he managed to find a piece of a branch with a sharp nub of twig projecting from it, which he made sharper. Whittling a groove around the top of the "hook," he unraveled the end of his shoelace and tied it tightly in the groove.

He held it up and looked at it appraisingly. He wouldn't bite on it, but then he wasn't a fish. Covered up with a large worm, it might not be so bad. Gimping down to a dry, shaded spot at the lake's edge, he cut a thin sapling, trimmed it, and tied on his line. So much for the fishing pole. Now for the bait.

With a flat, pointed stone for a shovel, he dug up a square of sod and began to turn up the soft earth underneath. He hit pay dirt almost at once—four or five fat nightcrawlers. He caught three and, for a moment, wondered what to do with them; shrugging, he tucked them gingerly into his shirt pocket.

Taking up his pole, he found a suitable fishing spot, where he impaled a worm on the hook, tossed it out into the still water, and sat down to wait. "Okay, worm, do your stuff."

His father would have claimed he was crazy, trying to catch fish in the middle of the day. "They'll all be holed up under some big snag," he'd have said.

Well, either Timothy found the right snag, or else the fish did things differently here, for within a few minutes he felt a sharp tug on the end of the pole. He yanked back, and frantically fumbled with the line, trying to pull it in. At first it was difficult; then suddenly the weight on the line was gone, and it floated slackly toward him.

When he drew it, dripping, from the water, he saw that the hook had been pulled off the line. "Crap!" He flung the pole down in the grass.

Something clammy touched his neck, making him jump. Startled, he brushed at it, and it tumbled to the ground. Just one of the worms. He retrieved it and looked about him for material for another hook. Not far off, he noticed some sort of thorny bush and he hobbled over to it. It proved to be covered with mean-looking scimitar-shaped thorns about half an inch long. Natural-made hooks. As he sat sawing away at a twig, trying not to puncture his fingers, he noticed, through the dense foliage in front of his face, something moving.

He let go of the thorny stem and peered around the edge of the bush. A hundred yards or less up the valley, near the mouth of the inlet, the bear was splashing around in the shallow water. At first it seemed that the animal was just playing, like a kid in a wading pool. But suddenly its paw swooped down and scooped up a great quantity of water—and something else, which sailed like a silvery football onto the bank. A fish.

The bear slogged out of the water and up the bank to where the fish flopped and struggled, and placed a huge paw on it. Without really thinking what he was doing, Timothy sprang up from behind the bush and yelled, "I want that fish!" The bear swung its head around slowly to stare at him, thrusting its face forward, seemingly trying to focus in on him, as if it were as nearsighted as Timothy himself.

"I'm hungry!" Timothy shouted, his voice cracking. "I want that fish! Now you . . . get!" Uncertainly, the bear backed up a few paces. "Go on!" Timothy called, desperately, waving one arm like he was shooing flies. As if just now grasping what this strange creature was trying to convey, the bear turned and shuffled obligingly off into the woods.

Timothy sank down into the grass, breathing hard. Boy, what a dumb thing to do! The bear could just as easily have decided to come after him, and then where would he be? Up the proverbial tree—except that there were no trees of any size for fifty yards around. And the questionable safety of the fire and the wooden spear lay clear across the meadow from him.

But the fact was, the tactic had worked—unless maybe the crafty bear was just waiting behind a tree until he came after the fish and then—pow! With this thought in mind, Timothy made a detour to the shelter for his spear before venturing to where the fish lay.

At first he thought it had flopped its way back into

the lake, but after a little looking he found it far back from the water, gasping its last gasps. He felt a stab of the same regret that had come over him when he killed —no, stunned, only stunned—the rabbit, but the hunger was more insistent; he picked the fish up by the tail and made off with it quickly, before he—or the bear—could change his mind.

He had seen his father clean fish enough times to have some idea of how to go at it. How to cook it was something else again. He settled on laying some green branches across the two chunks of wood he had used to support the water-boiling box. Scraping a bed of coals under them, he laid the fish atop the branches. It proved to be a fairly satisfactory method, except that it scorched some parts of the fish and left others almost raw. Besides that, the fish, some kind of sucker or carp, was rather oily and very bony. Still, Timothy wasn't about to complain; it was the first substantial food he'd had in—what?—four days? Five?

As he chewed on the fish, he tried to count up the days since he left camp, and came up with a total of seven. Had it really been a whole week? Somehow it seemed like less.

From the corner of his eye, Timothy noticed some movement, and he glanced toward the lake. The bear was wading out into the water to take up its fishing position again. Timothy smiled. "Thanks, friend," he called softly. As if in response to his call, the bear jerked its head up, whirled, and, sending up geysers of water, galloped out of the lake, across the strip of meadow, and into the trees. Timothy watched, bewildered. "What did I say?"

Then he heard the sound that had, in fact, alarmed the bear—a steady droning, like the hum of a huge insect. Timothy's heart began to race. "A plane!"

TWELVE

SHADING HIS EYES, he searched the sky frantically. When he saw the plane come into sight, over the treetops far up the valley, he dropped the fish and jumped to his feet, groaning as he put his weight on the sore one. Wildly, he flapped his arms. "Yooohhhh!" he shouted, though he knew there was no way he could be heard. "Over here! Over here!"

Instead of moving down the length of the valley, the plane headed across it; it wasn't even going to pass overhead. "Come on!" Timothy yelled. "I'm over here!" How could he catch the pilot's attention? A smoke signal! Hobbling about, he piled all the wood within reach onto the fire. It sent up a plume of smoke —but only because it was smothering. Torn between signaling the aircraft and keeping the fire alive, he hesitated; finally, he yanked most of the wood off again. Falling to his knees, he blew on the coals. "Come on, come on," he begged. Slowly, the flames began to reappear here and there. When he was sure it would go on burning, he threw back his head to look for the plane. There was no sign of it. He held very still and listened; he could barely hear a gnat-like buzz fading away.

Sighing despondently, he plunked himself down by the fire. He should have been prepared. He should have had some small green branches all piled up, ready to be tossed on the fire. Why didn't he ever think of those things? His father would have had two tons of green branches stacked neatly right next to the fire; so would Kevin.

Well, to look on the bright side, at least they didn't seem to have forgotten about him completely. Surely they'd keep on sending out planes until one spotted him. And he'd make sure they did spot him. Though it was too late in the day now, first thing in the morning he'd start gathering green wood.

Retrieving his fish from the dirt, he washed it off with a little boiled water and finished eating it, keeping his ears open just in case the plane might decide to fly over again. But all he heard was the crickets and frogs tuning up, and the occasional splash of a fish breaking the still surface of the water. All he saw was a beaver swimming around lazily near the dam, and a couple of white birds circling about and coming to rest in the weeds at the far edge of the lake.

The night was a cold one, and he roused himself twice to replenish the fire. He knew now not to try to make a bonfire, but to lay on only a few branches, just enough to keep the fire burning. Between these brief stirrings, he slept soundly and dreamed unremarkable dreams.

He woke early. The lake was nearly invisible, blanketed in mist. Without even leaving the shelter, Timothy reached out and laid some dampish wood on the fire and waited for it to kindle and warm him. When he tried to slip on his laceless hiking boots, the pain in his left foot made him cry out. Pulling off his sock carefully, he saw that the infection was worse than ever. The red lines that radiated from the puffy center had spread. The piddly little cut was turning into something serious—blood poisoning, maybe, or lockjaw. But what could he do about it? He recalled some movie he'd seen where the guy got gangrene in his foot and made the girl chop it off with an ax. Timothy shuddered. No way, even if he still had the ax.

Probably the best thing he could do was to stay off it. It was sort of a gloomy day anyway, a good day to just lie around and read. He could manage to make out the words well enough if he held the book close to his face. Actually, it wasn't so bad just lying there doing nothing at all, except watching the misty water and those animals whose life centered around it.

Funny to think how, not so long ago, he'd been puzzling over the lack of wildlife in the area. All you had to do, it seemed, was sit quietly and wait a little and the creatures would reveal themselves: The chipmunks, making their squeaky, birdlike noises; the unhurried, unperturbed turtles; the rabbits, alternating between frantic hopping and complete immobility; a fat muskrat or groundhog waddling a waving path through the tall grass.

A person could almost stand to stay here awhile, if he just had a little more food and some better water. Of course it wouldn't hurt to have some small diversion, like a few books, or maybe a radio. *Radio.* The word set off some alarm in his brain. "Oh, no," he murmured. He'd done another dumb thing, really dumb. He was sure of it.

His mind went back a week, to when he was sitting in the Jeep, trying to tune in the radio. He'd gotten the Montreal station, then he'd fiddled with the dial some more, then his father had called, and he'd turned down the volume. But he hadn't turned it off.

Suddenly Timothy knew why no search party had come for him in those first days—no one but his father had known he was lost. The car battery had, of course, run down, and there had been no way for his father to get to the ranger station except to walk. It was quite a distance; probably it would have taken him a whole day at least, maybe even two. By the time he returned with help, then, Timothy would have been nowhere near the place where he had first gotten lost. Dumb, dumb, dumb. If he'd just stayed put and waited, they probably would have had no trouble locating him.

On the other hand, the chances were he would have died of dehydration and exposure. As it was, he had things pretty much under control. When they finally did find him, he'd show them that, even though he might pull a stupid stunt from time to time, when the chips were down he could take care of himself and do just fine.

Of course, he didn't exactly look all that fine—his clothes were torn, his hair was tangled, and he was a little on the grungy side. But those things could be taken care of, too. He had rested long enough anyway.

He tossed a bunch of nuts into the coals to roast for lunch and then looked about for something to fashion a needle from. Spotting yesterday's fish bones, he set about picking over them until he found a long, thin, sharp one. Laboriously he drilled a hole through the thicker end with the small blade of his knife-fork-spoon. Then, pulling a thread from the frayed tail of his shirt, he worked it through the eye of the makeshift needle and proceeded to sew up the rent in his pants leg. It was no quick task, and when he was finally finished, it looked as though a blind man had done it, but at least his knee—which was all but healed now—no longer stuck out.

After lunch he tossed a little wood on the fire and hopped on one foot down to the edge of the lake, where he stripped off his clothes and washed them and himself thoroughly. Though the water was about the color of weak tea, it seemed clean enough. Probably the dark tint came from the leaves and tree bark and such that washed into the lake.

Timothy spread his wet clothing on the thorn bush to dry. Cutting a sizable thorn for a fish hook, he rounded up a worm and sat down on a flat rock with

---

his sore foot propped up on a hummock of grass, and gave his fishing tackle another try.

He drilled a hole, like the needle's eye, in the piece of thorn bush and tied the shoelace fishing line through it. This time it stayed on—securely enough to land some kind of perch, or maybe a bass, about as long as his foot. Wincing, he knocked it on the head with a rock, laid it behind him in the grass, and baited the hook again. But the fellow he'd caught must have been an orphan, or else suicidal, because there was no sign of a nibble after that.

Timothy laid the pole down. Clouds had crept over the sun and, feeling chilly, he pulled on his clothes, though they were still a little dampish. He glanced at his pitiful day's catch. There had to be some more efficient way of catching fish if you were interested in them as food and not as "sport." A net was beyond his capabilities. A trap, maybe, like a minnow trap? He had no way of constructing one, though. Maybe the bear had the right idea—chase them into a shallow pool and then grab them. Maybe he could even improve on the bear's method, make some kind of a funnel-type setup with rocks so that the fish could find their way in but not back out. When he could get around better, he'd work on it.

For now, he had to be content with frying the fish at hand. It proved to be less bony and more tasty than the one the bear had provided for him, and almost large enough to quiet his hunger for a while. Not that he couldn't have managed a jelly donut on top of it.

The sky had been partly overcast all day, but now it began to look positively threatening. Above the stark dead trees on the other side of the lake, it had turned purple and angry, like a giant bruise. It looked as if he was in for a real downpour. He'd better be prepared. Timothy grinned. The good old Boy Scout motto. If his father could only see him now.

On hands and knees he grubbed out a shallow trench uphill of the shelter, using a flat rock. It was exhausting work, and by the time he finished he was hungry again, and so tired that he felt like crawling inside his hut and calling it a day. But the roof needed work. He had repaired the framework of the shelter after the bear's visit, but had let the thatching go, since the weather had been good.

So now he had to scrabble about pulling up clumps of dead grass to stick in wherever he could see daylight through the thatch. When this task was done, he was really ready to drop. But something would have to be done about the fire. Though he probably had enough wood to last until morning, he had to keep it dry somehow. And if the rain was really heavy, how was he going to keep it from drowning the fire, which he had no way of rekindling? Build another roof over the fireplace? It seemed a little odd, but it might work if he made it high enough so it didn't catch fire.

Sighing, he got unsteadily to his feet and limped uphill into the woods. When he returned, he was dragging a couple of dead saplings. With them, he constructed a rather shaky lean-to directly over the fire, and roofed it with assorted sticks overlaid with bundles of grass and weeds, mostly green, to lessen the chance of its going up in flames. Another layer of sticks on top and the job was done—none too soon. Not only was he on the verge of collapsing, but the rain had already begun to announce itself with cold, scattered drops.

Blowing out his breath wearily, Timothy laid half the firewood inside his hut and crawled in after it. This survival stuff was certainly hard on a person. Still, along with the exhaustion he felt something even more pervasive, a deep sort of satisfaction.

It wasn't until he plumped up the down vest under his head and felt something square and solid that he realized he had gone through another whole day without so much as glancing at the book. And now it was too dark, and he was too tired anyway.

What had he done with the day? At home, he had so often been bored; here he had been disgusted, elated, exhausted, but never bored. Maybe the difference was that at home very little was expected of him, nothing required of him—and he had always done what was expected. If he ever did try to do anything more, it always turned out wrong. Someone could always do it better. Here, if something needed doing, either he did it or it didn't get done—and there was no one to say whether his way of going about it was right or wrong. It just either worked, or else it didn't—and sometimes it worked, and sometimes it didn't. Or, as the mountain men used to say, sometimes you ate the

bear, sometimes the bear ate you. And then again—
Timothy smiled, thinking of the berries, the fish, the
clams—then again, sometimes both you and the bear
ate the same things.

THIRTEEN

THE STORM TOOK ITS TIME in coming, but when it finally arrived it lived up to its advance notice, and then some. Timothy didn't have the energy to sit around waiting for it; he fell asleep, and was wakened in the dark by an apocalyptic thunderclap close at hand. He sat up abruptly, nearly sticking his head through the thatch. It sounded as if the sky were coming down around his ears. He swapped ends, so that he was facing the doorway of the shelter. The fire seemed to be surviving all right so far, despite an occasional gust of wind that swept rain across it and into Timothy's face. He shoved the water-boiling box out where it would catch some of the water, then retreated as far as he could into the shelter.

He had always liked watching the rain from his bedroom window at home, but there he had been so removed, so isolated from it. Here he felt the way he imagined wild animals must feel, holed up in a den or under some log, and grateful for the shelter. He had never been particularly aware of the roof over his head back home, any more than he was aware of the rest of his environment. The outdoors had been something you had to pass through to get to another heated, air-conditioned, closed-window building. There had been times when he went a whole day without even knowing what the weather was like outside—it didn't really matter.

To his father it mattered because, at least until they got a house closed in, it governed how much work got done. His father was always cursing the elements—the snow, the cold, the rain—as though they were the Enemy, with some personal vendetta against him. He built his houses with the haste of a commander erecting a fort. Yet he claimed to love the outdoors. But of course his fishing and hunting trips could be seen as battles in his war against nature, too. The first thing he always announced upon returning from the trip was the body count.

The rain continued all night. Timothy got up several times to tend the fire, and each time he lay awake awhile, listening to the rain's hypnotic cadence, augmented now and then by the hiss of drops in the fire, or by a roll of far-off thunder. A few drops sneaked through the thatching, but not enough to be a real nuisance, just enough to remind him of how wet he might have been.

The storm did not let up until late afternoon the next day. At last Timothy found a chance to open *Lord of the Flies* again. Oddly enough, after twenty or thirty pages he began to feel restless somehow, and a little impatient with the book. His mind kept wandering: Where did a bear go to sit out the rain? . . . He really ought to take a better look around the area—there might be wild grapes or berries. . . . How could he go about building that fish trap?

He dug a small piece of charcoal out of the ashes of the fire and began doodling possible fish-trap diagrams on the blank end-page of the book.

When the downpour tapered off at last, and the sun began to emerge, looking rather pale and washed-out, Timothy emerged, too. The air felt clean and stringent on his face, like his father's after-shave. First thing to do was gather more wood so it could dry by the fire. He rolled up his pants legs and actually took several steps through the wet grass before he felt a twinge in the infected foot. He had almost forgotten about it. Standing on one leg, he slipped off his left shoe and examined the sole of the injured foot. It looked far better. The swelling was still considerable, but the radiating red lines were shrinking. The enforced rest had done it good.

On his way back to the shelter with a large branch, he took a more circuitous route than usual and came upon another pleasant surprise—a patch of familiar-looking dark-green growth that, when he yanked some up by the roots, proved to have equally familiar bulbs at the end. Brushing the dirt off, he nibbled one to be certain. It was an onion, all right. He dragged the firewood on down to his camp and then returned to harvest some of the crop. As he bent over to pull up a handful of onions, he made yet another discovery.

Something glinting in the grass not far off caught his eye. What was there in nature that was shiny? Curious, he made his way to the spot. Not until he was right on top of it did he recognize the object, so totally out of place did it seem. Disgusted, he stooped and picked it up. A can. An aluminum beer can. Someone had been here before him, had probably hunted and fished and camped here. It might even have been his father, a long time ago.

"Crap." Timothy squeezed the sides of the can until they collapsed and then drew back his arm, meaning to fling the can as far away as he could—to the moon, if possible. Then he stopped and stared at it. Wait a minute. What was he doing? This wasn't just a beer can—it was a potential drinking cup, or a saucepan, maybe. Even if it was depressing to find it here, in what he had thought of as wilderness, he might just as well make use of it. It wasn't like he was trying to be some kind of purist or something, after all. He was trying to survive. It was just that . . . well, he'd had this feeling —like he was making it all on his own for a change, and this was sort of like depending on somebody else, in a way.

On the other hand, when you got right down to it, weren't you always dependent on somebody else for something? The ax, and the knife, the clothes he had on his back—they didn't grow on trees. Besides, he'd depended on the bear when it provided him with a fish; in fact, he was taking advantage of the fish themselves. So why not take advantage of a stray beer can?

In the end, he took the can back to camp with him, along with a handful of onions, and after carefully cutting the top out with his knife and pushing the sides back in place, he used it to boil up a sort of soup made of onions and the somewhat smelly remains of yesterday's fish. It wasn't Campbell's, but it wasn't too bad.

By the following day, he found he could walk almost normally, so he spent the early morning rounding up green branches to pile near the fire for use as a smoke signal. After that, he tried to catch a fish for lunch, with no success, and feasted instead on watery onion soup and the last of the nuts. After a long rest, during which he read and dried his dew-drenched boots by the fire, he set out on a trek around the perimeter of the lake. It proved to be a longer walk than he anticipated, for the land just below the beaver dam was swampy and he was forced to make a wide detour.

But it was worth the walk. In a brushy area on the far side of the lake, he found both a cranberry bush and a scraggly tree with a sprinkling of wild plums on it, most of which he ate greedily on the spot. As he stood wondering whether to use his shirt for a berry basket or go back for the birch box, he heard a distant humming sound that made his heart speed up suddenly. He held his breath and listened. The plane! "Oh, for crying out loud!" he wailed, and took off around the lake again, his laceless boots flopping.

He'd never make it. He knew he'd never make it. He kept trying to watch the sky as he ran and, as a result, sank almost up to his knee in a boggy spot and had to stop and fish his shoe out of the mire. In the pause, he noticed that the sound of the plane didn't seem to be getting any louder. He shaded his eyes and scanned the sky for a time before he spotted it, far down the valley —headed in some other direction.

"I hope you crash," he muttered after it. "You creep." He cleaned off his shoe by wading across the creek in it, and slogged back to camp. After debating awhile whether or not to wait by the fire in case the plane returned, he picked up the birch box and headed back around the lake. At least the cranberries were a sure thing.

As the days went by and his foot began to get back to normal, Timothy made more exploratory trips, but in none of them did he stray very far from the camp —partly because the plane might be back, partly out of fear of getting lost again. On nearly every trip he turned up some new source of food: another sort of nut tree; a glade thick with wild grapevines; a couple of good-sized puffballs. These last he remembered his father pointing out to him once. Still, having heard tales of poisonous mushrooms, he was wary and, after taking an experimental bite, waited a whole day without ill effects before he was convinced they were edible. In fact, they proved to be quite good when cooked with chunks of fish and wild onion.

He was working on constructing the fish trap, lug-

121

ging stones to fence off a shallow pool, when the plane returned. This time it was headed up the valley, toward him. Timothy dropped the stone he was carrying and hurried across the meadow to the shelter.

Since parts of the valley were quite narrow, the aircraft was flying high. Chances were it wouldn't see him, no matter how much he waved and jumped around, and from the air his shelter would undoubtedly look like just so much more dead grass. He was going to have to send up smoke if he expected the pilot to notice anything. Quickly, he piled on dry wood to build up the flames. By the time he got a good blaze going, the shadow of the plane was undulating along the valley floor, almost to the beaver dam. Timothy grabbed up a bunch of the green branches he had gathered and stood holding them in his arms.

He looked up, following the plane's progress for a moment. It seemed almost to be traveling in slow motion. Its shadow rippled leisurely over the beaver dam, then across the surface of the lake. Timothy still held the green wood poised over the fire.

The incessant drone of the plane's engine was like a nagging fly buzzing in his ears, and he frowned and shook his head slightly, as if trying to chase the insect away. When he glanced up again, the plane was directly overhead. Still he didn't drop the armful of branches; he kept hold of them while the plane's shadow climbed one wall of the valley, fluttered across the treetops, and over the crest of the hill. In a few moments, the plane itself dwindled and disappeared, and, finally, Timothy lost track of the insistent hum of the engine.

FOURTEEN

IN THE DAYS THAT FOLLOWED, the plane did not fly over again. Either they had stopped looking for him, or they were doing it somewhere else or some other way. Timothy didn't give much thought to the matter, because when he thought about people searching for him it made him think of his mother. She was the one person who might miss him. Still, it wasn't like he'd never been away from her before. He was gone longer than this to summer camp—except for last year, when he got tonsillitis and had to come home a week early.

That was the one thing, aside from his mom, that worried him about staying here: that he might take really sick, with no doctor around. But the fact was, now that the knee and the foot were mostly mended, he felt really good. Oh, he woke up with a stiff neck and an aching back most mornings from the sleeping accommodations, but that worked itself out. He never experienced that overall, unspecific, washed-out feeling he got so often back home, which his mother, in her written excuse to his school, generally called "a touch of the flu."

He'd even lost some of the extra weight his father was always harping at him about. One day when he slipped on his jeans beltless, after having rinsing them out, they promptly slid down around his hips. It used to be his pants were a little on the tight side, even without a belt. Sometimes he'd even had to leave the snap at the waist undone.

Surprisingly, though, he wasn't hungry all the time, the way he'd been at first, either because his stomach had shrunk or because he was getting better at scrounging food—or both.

After some experimentation, he had mastered the art of trapping fish: With his boots on to protect his feet, he waded out into the lake as far as he could, and then splashed ostentatiously across the muddy bottom toward the funnel-like rows of rocks he had laid up. Generally he herded at least half a dozen fish of all sizes before him, which swam between the narrowing walls, through a small gap, and into the shallow pool beyond, where he scooped them up much as the bear had done. What he couldn't eat right away, he cleaned and cut into strips and smoked over the fire.

During one of these fish roundups, he felt a sudden awareness of some presence besides his own in the vicinity, and he lifted his head to scan the surroundings anxiously. At first he saw nothing, except a beaver sitting atop its lodge, sunning itself. Then he heard a faint snuffling noise and glanced toward the woods just above him.

The bear stood at the edge of the trees, watching him placidly. Timothy felt a quick, involuntary stab of fear. He had never seen the animal this close before. Funny, though; it wasn't nearly as big as he would have guessed, not much larger than himself, really. It was just fatter, and a lot more furry. Unsure what to do, Timothy slogged slowly backward a few steps and then circled around to the bank just below the thorn bush. The bear didn't even seem to be watching him; it had its eye on his fish corral. When Timothy had retreated all the way to his camp, the animal gave him one glance, then padded to the edge of the water for a closer look.

Seeing the trapped fish, it waded in and leisurely placed a big paw on one; it bent to grab the fish in its jaws, splashed back to solid ground, and ambled off into the trees. Timothy shook his head, amazed and amused. "Okay," he called after the bear. "Fair is fair."

Unfortunately, the bear didn't confine his visits to the fish-catching pool. A couple of days later, Timothy returned from a nut-gathering foray to find his fish-drying rack knocked to the ground and cleared of fish, and his berry basket mangled and, of course, quite empty.

"Now this," he announced loudly and angrily, in case the bear should be within earshot, "is going too far." He had counted on the presence of the fire to keep animals at a distance, but evidently it was too small, or else the bear had simply grown used to it.

After that, Timothy dug a hole to store his food in, and when he left camp for any length of time, he slid a good-sized rock over the top of it. This either fooled the bear or discouraged it, for he had no trouble after that.

Considering how simple and streamlined his way of life had become, there never seemed to be any lack of things to do. If he wasn't foraging for food, he was experimenting with some new idea he'd come up with. He spent several days gathering clay from the riverbank just above the inlet, working the stones out of it, and shaping it into a crude pot—which proceeded to develop huge cracks in its surface as it dried. Another day was taken up with weaving a basket from cattail fronds —which subsequently dried out and shrunk, leaving large gaps in the shell of the basket. There was always firewood to be rounded up, of course, for the nights were turning positively cold.

The days were still mostly clear and sunny, though the sun was noticeably lower in the sky than it had been a couple of weeks before. The shadows at midday seemed long and somehow insubstantial. It seldom got so warm now that he felt comfortable going shirtless, and he didn't feel like bathing often in the chilly lake.

After one particularly crisp, clear day and the frigid night that followed, he woke in the morning to find a veil of white frost spread on the grass. It melted off as soon as the sun rose, but it had done its work. Patches of weeds turned abruptly from green to brown, and here and there on the hillsides, a few maples turned brilliant red overnight.

As the plums and berries began to overripen and drop or shrivel up, Timothy started to look elsewhere for food. He tried everything that he had ever remotely heard of being edible, and some that he hadn't but which looked as if they might be: dandelions, milkweed, cattails, grass seed, thistledown, crabapples, turtles, frogs, rose hips. He considered trying to devise a snare out of his shoelaces or some such thing but, remembering his earlier experience with the rabbit, he decided against it. He wasn't that hungry yet.

Of course, when you got right down to it, fish and turtles and frogs were very much living things, too, and he did feel a little sorry and a little squeamish about taking their lives. But he felt he had to draw the line somewhere, or he'd have to forgo eating plants as well, because *they* were alive.

On the whole, he managed to remain fairly well fed and reasonably warm, though keeping himself in food and firewood sometimes occupied a large part of his day. But at least he was never bored. After he got through *Lord of the Flies,* he found himself wishing for another book to read in that comfortable, drowsy space between supper and sleep. Mostly, though, it was a brief period anyway, for he was usually so tired out from the day's various tasks and hikes that he couldn't have stayed awake for even the most compelling book ever written. Usually he fell asleep watching the sun set.

He had no idea any longer how many days he had been "lost". One day passed into another so seamlessly that he had stopped counting. Why bother, really? He had no appointments to keep, no holidays to observe. He knew it was well into September by now, and that his school must surely be back in session.

When this first occurred to him, he felt a certain uneasiness, a conditioned guilt, as if he were playing hooky and would be held accountable. He even worried a little about missing some important topic and not being able to catch up on his return. On the other hand, when he had been present there had never seemed to be anything very important going on.

It never really crossed his mind that he might not return. Somewhere in the back of his mind, he kept the vague intent, if no one came to find him, of going on to follow the course of the river, as originally planned, until he came to civilization of some description. It was just that he was not in any particular hurry to start.

This was civilization enough, at least for the time being. He had everything he needed here, except for maybe a decent water supply—and that, too, was not long in coming.

One warm and hazy afternoon, he ranged farther than usual on one of his exploratory hikes, following the ridge that overlooked the river. As he moved downstream, the ground grew steeper and rockier until, perhaps a mile from his camp, it began to fall away in sheer cliffs, some of which rose fifteen or twenty feet above

129

the nearly level flood plain below. As he stood admiring the view, Timothy heard a faint trickling sound somewhere beneath his feet. Getting down onto his belly at the edge of the drop-off, he stuck his head over and looked down. Ten feet below him, a tiny stream of water issued from the rocks and immediately disappeared into a large, lush patch of moss and ferns and other foliage. It wasn't a strong enough flow to have cut a path to the river, but seemed instead to soak into the ground.

Timothy scanned the face of the cliff and, seeing a cleft that made a sort of sloping passageway down to the base of the rocks, he half climbed, half slid down it. When he stood on level ground, the miniature spring was not even visible behind all the greenery. But when he walked forward and parted the bushes, he saw a wispy ribbon of water winding down the face of the rock.

He cupped his hand under it and drank the few drops he collected. The water was cold and tasteless. He sat back and cupped his chin in his hand thoughtfully. Obviously, he wasn't going to catch much of the water the way things stood. What he was going to need was some kind of a collecting basin at the foot of the cliff—maybe just a hole dug out and lined with clay dug from the river.

When he had lunched on a lump of the "white man's pemmican" he had invented—roasted nuts and dried berries pounded together with smoked fish—he set to work digging up the wet earth with a flat rock.

After a few minutes of fighting with the mud, he turned his attention to diverting the tiny stream temporarily by means of strategically placed rocks, so he could proceed without getting drenched.

Two or three weeks ago, he would have had to stop and rest ten minutes for every five minutes' work. Now he dug steadily, stopping only briefly to catch his breath and wipe the sweat from his forehead, until the hole was nearly two feet across and maybe a foot and a half deep. Blowing out his breath, he stood and moved back a few steps to assess his handiwork.

"Find anything?" said a voice. Timothy whirled around, his eyes wide, his heart pounding.

FIFTEEN

"DIDN'T MEAN TO SCARE YOU, KID." A few paces away stood two men, dressed nearly alike in work pants, flannel shirts, bright orange vests, and red hunters' caps. Both carried rifles; one held his under his armpit, while the other's was laid casually across his shoulder. They seemed to be looking him over as thoroughly as he was them.

The shorter one scratched his day's growth of beard and said, "What you digging for, worms?"

Timothy had trouble finding his voice. "No," he said, finally, faintly. He felt like running, but he had an unreasonable, unsettling fear that they would fire on him if he did, out of pure hunting instinct.

"You out here all by your lonesome?" asked the other one, a tall, skinny, red-haired man. "Where's your folks?"

"I—they—" Timothy swallowed hard. "Upriver a ways."

"Fishing, are they?"

"Ah . . . no. Just . . . camping."

"You don't suppose"—the shorter one grinned—"they'd have an extra cup of coffee? It's quite a ways back to our camp."

"No! I mean . . . they don't drink coffee."

The two hunters looked at one another questioningly, then back at Timothy. "What's your trouble, son?" the taller one said. "You're acting kind of spooky. Anything wrong?"

"No."

The man frowned, apparently unconvinced. "Well, tell you what. We'll walk you on back to your camp, okay?"

There was no way out of it. He'd said the camp lay upstream, so he couldn't very well lead them off in some other direction. He headed slowly, reluctantly, up the riverbank, and the hunters fell in behind him like some sinister armed guard.

They walked in silence for some time, their feet swishing in the long grass. Finally, as much for a reason to check on them as anything, Timothy half turned and, glancing at their shouldered guns, said, "What—what are you hunting for?"

The shorter one slapped the stock of his rifle and grinned. "Bear," he said.

It seemed like no time at all before the beaver dam came in sight ahead of them. Though Timothy tried to walk as slowly as he could, before long they had rounded the end of the lake and his camp at the edge of the woods was in full view.

In the weeks he had been living there, the place had become so familiar to him that he no longer thought about how it looked, any more than he had thought about how the house in Elmira looked when he was there. It served his purposes, that was all.

Now he seemed to suddenly see it with new eyes, like a person coming upon it for the first time—perhaps as it must look to the two hunters. How it looked was shabby and rather pitiful. How could he have thought he was making it so civilized? There was a crooked little structure that looked like nothing more than a pile of sticks and grass; there was a trampled area in front of it strewn with twigs and bark; a heap of charred wood and ashes from which a thin plume of smoke rose; a couple of unidentifiable items made of bark and clay; a shaky frame made of sticks; an empty turtle shell . . . and that was all.

Timothy halted, feeling somehow defeated and ashamed, not wanting the hunters to ask questions or to poke around at his stuff, maybe have a good laugh over his crude attempts at bushcraft.

"This is it?" the shorter man said, incredulously. "This is your camp?"

Timothy nodded slightly, unable to speak.

The taller one looked around. "Where's the rest of your family?" When Timothy didn't answer, the man clamped a hand on his shoulder and turned him so they were facing. "Look, what's the story here? Do your folks know where you are? What'd you do, run off?"

"No!"

"What then? Are you lost?"

Timothy shrugged. There didn't seem to be much point in staying on now, even if they let him. It just wouldn't be the same. "Yeah," he murmured.

"Well, why didn't you say so before? How long've you been lost?"

"I don't know. Since about the last week of August."

The shorter man whistled. "Over three weeks. And no gun or anything? What the heck did you live on?"

Timothy shrugged again. "Stuff. Look, are you going to take me back, or what?"

"Sure, kid, sure. We're just camped down the river a few miles. We'll take you to the nearest ranger station. I bet they've been doing some searching for you." He glanced at the fire. "You should've kept a signal fire going."

"Come on, Larry," the taller man said. "He's just a kid. You can't expect him to think of everything. He's lucky he's even alive." The tall hunter clapped Timothy's shoulder again. "Speaking of fires, we'd better douse that one before we leave."

"I'll get it," Larry said and, before Timothy could protest, he stirred the coals around and sprinkled dirt over them carefully, like a man tossing earth on a grave.

"Anything you want to take along?" the tall man asked.

Timothy glanced desolately about a moment at the little camp, then lifted his eyes and slowly took in the whole of the landscape around him: the green hills, spotted now with gold and scarlet, reflected in the still water; the lush grass of the meadow; the dead trees like a row of stark sculptures on the far edge of the lake. He half hoped to catch some final glimpse of wildlife—a beaver paddling about near the dam, a white bird coming to rest in the weeds—but every living thing seemed to have gone into hiding from the intruders. Perhaps it was just as well. He wouldn't want any animal here to be a target for the two hunters. Still, it seemed unfair somehow to have to leave so abruptly, without anyone or anything to see him go. But then maybe, somewhere up the valley, at the edge of the woods, hidden within the shadow of the trees, there might well be a furry black shape watching curiously as he and the two men turned away and started downriver.

"I said, is there anything you wanted to take along?"

Timothy shook his head slowly. How could he tell them that he wanted to take it all? "No," he said, simply. "Nothing."

When they came to the lower end of the lake, abreast of the beaver dam, Timothy fell back behind the others a few steps; he chose a moment when they were not looking to turn and wave once, quickly, in farewell.

SIXTEEN

THE HUNTERS' CAMP looked like the cover off an L. L. Bean catalog, complete with tautly erected umbrella tent and tightly rolled sleeping bags, spotless Coleman stove and lantern, self-contained washbasin, and aluminum mess kits. Timothy even spotted, on the folding table next to the stove, a collapsible drinking cup. He smiled secretly, smugly. These guys weren't fooling around. If they were going to camp in the wilderness, by golly, they were going to do it right.

Their transportation was no less magnificent—a brand-new four-wheel-drive truck. It looked as incongruous sitting in the middle of the logging trail as those cars in the commercials, where they set them up on the peak of a mountain.

He had to admit, though, that it was comfortable inside as they bounced along the road back to civilization. Timothy almost felt as if he shouldn't touch the clean, smooth upholstery. He was suddenly aware of how grungy he must appear, with his tangled hair and rumpled, torn clothing.

The hunters kept plying him with questions, to which he gave mostly monosyllabic answers. After a while they gave up and talked between themselves about their plans for the next day's hunt. Timothy sat pressed against the passenger door, half tempted to open it and jump out. He felt the way he imagined a captured animal must feel.

After a few miles, the logging trail intersected with a regular dirt road, which they roared down, leaving a cloud of brown dust in their wake. It was still quite a long while before they delivered him to the ranger station. The headquarters was a rustic cabin of dark-stained logs, but inside it proved to be as clean and bright and modern as the house in Elmira. Even the ranger who greeted them was clean and bright, and very average-looking—he looked, in fact, like something out of the pages of L. L. Bean's catalog, too. "How can I help you gentlemen?"

Timothy had hung back as close to the entrance as possible, but the tall hunter put an arm around his shoulders and urged him forward. "We caught this critter alive and thought we'd turn him in."

Frowning, the ranger slowly circled his desk and half-crouched in front of Timothy to look him in the eye. "What's your name, son?"

"Tim."

The ranger's eyes widened. "Timothy Martin?" Timothy nodded reluctantly. The ranger straightened and scratched his head. "Well, I'll be—" Over his shoulder he called, "Hey, Willis! Come on in here!"

A second ranger, stockier and more rumpled-looking, emerged from a back room with a cup of coffee in his hand. "What's up?"

"Guess who we got here."

"Good Lord." The ranger named Willis nearly dropped his cup. "The Martin kid?" He handed the coffee to Timothy. "Here. You need this more than I do."

"No, thanks," Timothy said.

"Well, how about a candy bar, then?" He pulled a Snickers off a wire rack and thrust it into Timothy's hand. "There. You must be about starved to death."

"Not really." Timothy unwrapped the end of it and nibbled at it, just to be polite, but had trouble swallowing it.

The ranger named Willis stared at him, as if he'd never seen a boy eat a candy bar before. "Isn't this something? We thought for sure you'd be— Well, that is, we'd just about given up on you."

"We figured you'd probably know who he was," the shorter of the two hunters said.

"You figured that right." The first ranger laughed. "We've had an all-out search on for this young fellow for the past three weeks. You maybe missed it, being from out of state, but his picture's been on every TV station and every newspaper in the area. We had airplanes out looking for him, we had bloodhounds; we even had a psychic up here trying to pinpoint his

---

139

whereabouts on the map." The ranger tousled Timothy's hair in mock exasperation, beneath which Timothy sensed a layer of real exasperation, perhaps at all the trouble he'd caused them. Timothy couldn't help feeling, secretly and perversely, a little proud, the way he used to feel when he and Kevin would play hide and seek and he hid so well that Kevin had to call him in; sometimes he had refused to reveal himself even then, not wanting to divulge his hiding place, in case he might need to use it again.

"Where in the devil have you been hiding all this time?" the ranger was saying.

Timothy shrugged. "No place."

When the hunters had gone, the rangers put a call through to the local police, to inform them of his safe return, then one to Timothy's parents. When they put Timothy on the line, he had trouble thinking of anything to say.

"Timmy?" His mother's voice sounded choked-up and unfamiliar. "Timmy? Are you there?"

"Yeah, Mom. I'm here."

"Thank God! Oh, Timmy! We were so worried! It's been so long! We thought—we were afraid . . . are you all right?"

"Sure, I'm okay."

"Are you sure? You're not hurt, or sick? You sound —I don't know . . . different."

I am, he wanted to say, but didn't. "I'm . . . okay," he repeated.

"Thank God. Now, you stay right where you are;

we'll be up to get you as soon as we can. I'll call your father and we'll leave right away. Now, you stay right there, you understand?"

"You really don't need to come; I could take a bus, or—"

"Oh, honey, don't be silly. You've been through a terrible ordeal. You just rest. We'll be up just as soon as we can. Do they have food for you there?"

"Of course. I'm eating a Snickers right now."

"All right. All right, let me talk to the man again, so I can get directions. You're sure you're not hurt or anything?"

"No. I'm okay."

"Well, thank God. We were so worried. If it had been Kevin, we— Well, never mind. The important thing is that you're safe. We'll see you soon. Let me talk to the man, now."

Apparently his mother was not fully convinced of his ability to assess his own condition, for after the catalog-model ranger took over the receiver, he heard the man saying, "Not bad, really, considering how long he's been out. A little . . ." He glanced at Timothy. " . . . a little wild-looking, but he seems healthy enough."

Wild-looking. Timothy found his way to the wash-room and, leaning on the sink, he peered into the mirror. The face that looked back was only vaguely familiar. Where was the pale, slightly pudgy, slightly pimpled person with glasses who had made disapproving faces at him for so many years? This new fellow was not what you might call handsome, but he had a nice tanned complexion and a firm chin, and his shaggy hair, though a little unkempt, was not unbecoming.

Hearing someone approaching, he hurriedly turned on the tap and began scrubbing his hands with a cake of soap. The catalog ranger stuck his head through the doorway. "There's a shower in the utility room."

"That's okay."

"Just thought you might want to get civilized. Your folks ought to be here in about . . . four or five hours, I'd say."

Out of old habit, Timothy glanced at his watch. It still said five-twenty, just as it had for weeks. He unbuckled the strap and tossed the watch in the wastebasket. "It's almost five-thirty," the ranger said. So, the watch, by pure coincidence, had been nearly correct. It was almost as if he hadn't been gone at all, as if time had stopped while he was absent and was only now resuming its flow. "We'll be having supper in a half-hour or so. I imagine you'll be plenty hungry."

Timothy shrugged. "I had a big lunch."

He ate a little anyway, but was careful not to over-load his shrunken stomach, passing on the roast beef, and concentrating on the mashed potatoes and peas. He had found himself missing potatoes more than any other food in these past weeks. There must be something a person could substitute for them in the wild. After dinner, he'd have to see if the station had a book about wild foods.

The two rangers occupied the mealtime by filling him in on the details of the search, to which he only half listened. He did gather that he had been right about the run-down Jeep battery. His father hadn't shown up at the nearest ranger station until four days after Timothy failed to come back to camp; two days he had spent searching on his own, and two more walking out of the woods. Apparently he had hung around a couple more days, but when they still had found no trace of Timothy the rangers had sent him home, promising to do all they could and to keep him posted.

The search, as the ranger had indicated, had been quite intense, at least in the first week; but when even the bloodhounds had been stymied—because of the bear's scent over Timothy's, they figured—they had concentrated on an air search.

The story of their efforts was followed by a team lecture on how to avoid getting lost, and what to do if you did. The gist of it was that you should stay put. Timothy listened dutifully and without comment. Even if he had been vitally interested in what they had to say, the effectiveness would have been undermined by the fact that the phone kept ringing.

The rangers took turns answering it. Each time it was another television or radio station, or a newspaper, all wanting to know the facts about Timothy's "ordeal" and "rescue." Several of the reporters asked to talk to Timothy himself; he declined, letting the ranger explain that he was still too traumatized by the experience to talk about it.

When he had finished eating, he asked Willis if

there were any books around that he could read.
"Well," the ranger said, doubtfully, "I don't think
there's much that a kid would like. But I guess you can
take a look if you want to."

As he had hoped, there was a volume on edible wild
plants, and Timothy sat absorbed in it, trying to ignore
the ringing of the phone and the repeated explanations
of the rangers, until he saw a car with a plastic sign
reading MARTIN CONSTRUCTION CO. pull up into the
circle of light cast by the vapor lamp outside. He
watched as his parents got out and climbed the front
steps. They looked worse than he did, really, tired and
disheveled from their rushed trip. For the first time it
occurred to him that maybe the past weeks had been
an ordeal for them as well.

His mother began looking around anxiously the moment she stepped through the front door. When she
spotted Timothy by the window, she started to cry.
Hurrying to him, she threw her arms around him even
before he was completely out of his chair. Embarrassed,
Timothy pulled away a little, mumbling, "I told you I
was okay, Mom."

"Oh, but look at you; you poor thing. You look so
thin. Just look at your hair. And your glasses—where
are your glasses?"

"Broken. I can manage without them."

His father had held back a bit, talking to the catalog
ranger. Now he approached, almost reluctantly, seem-
ing somehow awkward and at a loss for words. "Glad
you made it back in one piece," he said finally. "We

were starting to get worried." He patted Timothy's shoulder briefly. "I tried to tell your mother you'd be all right, that there was plenty of water around, and that a person can go for a month easy without food—especially if they have some fat reserves." Now Timothy's stomach got a pat. "Looks like you used up some of the reserves."

"Yeah," Timothy said. Without even knowing he was going to say it, he added, "Why'd you go home?"

His father blinked and started to reply, then hesitated as if trying to formulate a better answer. "Well . . ." he said. "There was really nothing more I could do here. Finding people is these fellows' job. I had my own job to get back to."

"Your father did look for you for two whole days, honey," his mother added. "He did his best."

"I'd have found you, too, if you'd stayed in one place. And I'd have had help a lot sooner, if I'd had a car that ran."

"Jerry," his mother said, with a smile that was tight at the edges. "Let's just be glad he's home safe and sound." She hugged Timothy's shoulders. "I guess you'd like to go home now, and have some decent food, and sleep on a bed for a change, huh?"

Timothy nodded. "I guess so." He still held the book on edible plants, opened to Jerusalem artichokes. He glanced at it, then held it out reluctantly to Willis. "Where could I get one of these?"

The ranger laughed and shrugged. "You can have that copy if you really want it, son."

"What—?" His mother took the book and read the title. "Why on earth would you want such a thing?" she asked, with a nervous laugh.

The catalog ranger laughed, too—why was everyone laughing? "In case he gets lost again, I guess. He wants to be prepared."

"Well," his father said, just as Timothy figured he would, "you know, that's the Boy Scout motto."

SEVENTEEN

THE DRIVE HOME was as silent as if Timothy had been some stranger—a hitchhiker, perhaps. No one seemed to want to talk about his "lost" time. It was just as well; it would only have turned into a lecture, anyway, about why he'd done this and why he hadn't done that.

Once, not long after they started, he noticed his father glancing repeatedly at him in the rearview mirror, as though to make sure he was still there. But all his father said was, "What about the ax?"

"Jerry!" his mother admonished. "How can you worry about such a thing now?"

"I wasn't worried. I just wondered if we'd left it behind."

"I left it," Timothy said. "In the woods."

"Oh."

When they reached Utica, his mother made his father stop at Burger King and, despite Timothy's contention that he really wasn't hungry, she bought him a Whopper and fries. Though he managed to get it all down, under his mother's watchful eye, in half an hour he was feeling distinctly sick at his stomach. He lay back on the seat for a while.

The ride seemed endless. When his insides began to feel less troubled, he sat up and stared out at the passing landscape, or as much of it as he could see; it was dark and nearly featureless, except for an occasional house light. After a time, he said casually, "Did anybody ask about me? From school or anything?"

"Ask about you?" His mother laughed. For a moment, Timothy believed it was because he had been so stupid as to think that anyone at school cared what happened to him. Then she went on. "They never stopped! The principal has called several times, and all your teachers, and your friends—"

"What friends?" Timothy said, but she did not seem to hear.

"And the reporters!" she cried, clapping a hand to her forehead. "They practically camped out on our doorstep!" She turned and stared at him a long moment, as if making sure that it was really him. "You're practically a celebrity, you know."

Timothy lay back again, feeling uncomfortable. A celebrity? Just because he had wandered off and got himself lost? "What about Kevin?" he asked.

"Oh, he was every bit as worried as we were. Do you know, he wanted to take off from school to go and help search for you?"

"He did?"

"Uh-huh. We decided it would be best if he didn't. After all, what if he had gotten lost, too?"

Timothy sniffed. "He wouldn't."

"Oh, now, I don't know. Your father even admitted that he got himself a little lost out there, while he was looking for you. Didn't you, Jerry?"

His father laughed, without much humor. "Well, not so much *lost*, exactly. It was more like I was . . . what was it Dan'l Boone used to say? I was—I was *bewildered* once there for a couple of hours."

Timothy stared out again at the dark hills, which were barely distinguishable from the blackness of the sky. Bewildered. That was a good word. Now that he thought about it, it might well come from the same root as the word "wilderness." If a person looked at it that way, it didn't necessarily have a negative connotation at all; it could just mean you were overwhelmed, or maybe overcome, like in the word "besotted," or "becalmed," or "bedazzled." So he could, when asked, truthfully say that he hadn't actually been lost at all— only overcome by the wilderness.

The funny thing was, nobody asked him about how or why he got lost. What they wanted to know—all the TV reporters and newspaper people that swarmed around their house in the next few days—was how he survived. He told them, as simply as he could. They all seemed amazed at his ingenuity and fortitude.

Timothy felt like telling them that he had not done anything so amazing; he had just blundered along,

---

149

doing some things right and some things wrong, just the way anybody would do. That was enough for him: that he had done what anybody would do. But he knew they didn't want to hear that.

There were a lot of other things he didn't tell them, too—things he felt they would not understand, that he wasn't sure he understood himself, that he didn't even tell to his parents.

Not that they asked, anyway. When they eventually came around to talking about the episode, they only recounted what had gone on here at home: how his mother had refused to stir out of the house, for fear of missing the call that said he had been found; how they had imagined all sorts of dire things happening to him; how people they hadn't seen in years had phoned, asking what they could do to help.

But they never seemed to get around to asking what really did befall him in those lost weeks. Perhaps they still assumed, like the ranger, that it had been a traumatic experience for him and that, like some shell-shocked battle veteran, he would prefer not to talk about it.

In that, they were right. He didn't much feel like talking about it. But he spent a long time each day alone in his room, writing down in a journal all that he could remember about his weeks of "bewilderment."

By the time he had been home a week, the media's curiosity had been satisfied and life had returned to normal, or at least nearly enough so that Timothy could start to school again without running a gauntlet of cameras and microphones on the way.

But at school he was set upon all over again. He had not even made it as far as the office before two of his classmates—whose conversations with him in the past had been limited to derogatory remarks about his appearance—waylaid him. One thumped him soundly on the back. "Hey, Kit Carson! Glad to see you're back." The other slapped his chest. "Yeah, and your front, too!" They laughed loudly but seemingly without malice. Timothy tried to smile, assuming that this was their concept of being friendly. "Thanks," he said.

The principal, too—once he realized who Timothy was—was effusive in his welcome, and his praise for Timothy's "extraordinary courage." He was, the principal said, a credit to the school. Timothy began to long for the anonymity of the classroom.

But even there he was not safe. Each teacher, without fail, insisted on making him recount his inspiring story. It had become, by now, nothing more than a recitation he was required to rattle off, like "Stopping by Woods on a Snowy Evening"—something he seemed to have learned by memorizing, rather than actually living through it.

Mr. Prosser, who was in his leisure time a Scoutmaster, volunteered him to speak at the next Scout meeting, even promising him a merit badge in Wilderness Skills.

When lunchtime came, Timothy made his way to the last table in the cafeteria, hoping to find a spot to himself and some time to think about what was happening. It was all so overwhelming, this sudden wave of attention sweeping over him. Before he had finally gotten up the nerve to take swimming lessons this past summer, he had spent more of his vacation days than he cared to remember on the swimming beach at the State Park, sitting on his Garfield towel on the hot sand, burning but never tanning, watching loud and lean boys, and girls still sporting baby fat, dunking and splashing one another, and he had wondered to himself what it must be like to be in the swim of things, as it were—to fit in so casually, so effortlessly.

He had never suspected that, in order to belong, you had to pay a price: you had to give something of yourself to anyone who asked. It was not, then, apparently, so effortless as it had seemed.

His thoughts were interrupted by Annette Costello —who had once written the wrong name ("To Jim") in his yearbook—plopping down next to him at the table. "So," she said. "How does it feel to be eating real food again?"

In History class, Mrs. Warner was not content, as his other teachers had been, to let him off with the condensed version of his wilderness adventure. She insisted —good-naturedly, of course—that he take her place before the class and give them a full accounting. How often, after all, she pointed out, did they have someone in their midst who had actually led a Stone Age existence?

Sighing, Timothy shuffled to the front of the room and turned to face the class. Some of the faces were eager; some who had been present in his other classes were clearly getting a little bored. He shifted from one foot to the other. "Well . . ." he began, slowly, reluctantly. "There's not much to tell."

As he tried to think of what he wanted to say, he let his gaze float over the heads of the class and focus on the back wall, where a large, multicolored map of New York State hung precariously from thumbtacks. Timothy stared at it raptly, as though he had never really seen it before.

An orange-headed pin was stuck in the map, near the bottom edge, in the exact center of the irregular blob that represented Elmira. Timothy's eyes traveled upward from this pin, northward, to the faint blue line that enclosed the great square of the Adirondack Park. He searched the northwest quadrant of the park, looking for some landmark, some indicator that would identify the place where he had been. It was impossible, at this distance, to tell. But he went on standing there, as if in a trance, ignoring the teacher's promptings, just staring at the map, the way he had so often studied the imaginary country that lay among the cracks of his bedroom ceiling, wishing himself there.

AUTHOR'S NOTE

WILD TIMOTHY is a work of fiction and not meant to be a Wilderness Survival Manual. Timothy did some things right but, since he was working by trial and error, he also did a lot of things wrong. While all the wild foods mentioned are edible in one form or another, some require preparation to be on the safe side. Clams, for example, shouldn't be eaten raw, because they can contain parasites. Springs, even in relatively unpopulated areas, are seldom totally unpolluted. If you want to know more about wild foods and survival techniques, there are a number of good nonfiction books on the subject available through your library, bookstore, or county extension service.